DULCE BASE
The Dulce Files, Book One

GREG STRANDBERG

Big Sky Words Press, Missoula

Copyright © 2014 by Greg Strandberg

Big Sky Words

First paperback printing, 2015

Printed in the United States of America

ISBN: 1508519153
ISBN-13: 978-1508519157

CONTENTS

PRELUDE – LEVEL 2

Dulce Base – Dulce, New Mexico
Friday, May 1, 1975

Reggie Copeland hated Dulce Base, hated being underground, and hated being away from his trailer with its TV and fridge full of cold beer. He hated Mount Archuleta and meant to get out the first damn chance he got, and *had* been meaning to since he'd turned 18 nearly two decades earlier.

He frowned and slumped over the steering wheel of the large dump truck, one with tires fifteen feet high. *What the hell else am I going to do?*

As usual, Reggie had woken up about an hour before his 9 PM shift started, or more appropriately, came-to from passing out on the floor the night before, which was his typical evening procedure, although it took place before noon. After pulling himself together, finishing off a Coors, and dragging a comb through the tangled mat he called his hair, Reggie'd climbed into the cab and gotten onto U.S. Route 64, passed the one motel and one gas station that the small, sleepy town of Dulce (pop. 900) afforded, and drove the 2.5 miles to the base.

Everyone knew Reggie, and the gates in the barbed-wire fence were opened to him and he rumbled on in, headed down the road, and reached the large tan and featureless garage. They were waiting for him – or at least that evening's shift change – and he trundled the truck right on in the open garage doors, which were large enough to accommodate a Boeing 747.

The garage was just that – a large garage where everyday base vehicles were repaired. It was a huge floor measuring more than 100,000 square feet, or about the size of two football fields. The place was currently full of vehicles being serviced, as it always was, though Reggie knew that sometimes it housed more. That's why it was often call the port, a name given to ships, even though it was in the middle of the desert.

1

Further back there was another set of garage doors, these much thicker and with an additional set of guards stationed at them, each with a loaded machine gun in their hands. They were the HUB doors, or what Reggie typically thought of as nuclear blast doors, and it was here that he slowed down and had a scanner put over his face, which was nothing more than some red light that passed over his face in a long narrow strip. It fed something back to the two guards and the small hand-held calculator-like thing they had, and then Reggie was waved through, just like the hundreds of times before, maybe thousands now. It wasn't that they needed the thing – the small, black teardrop tattoo on Reggie's right cheek set him apart from everyone else on the base – but it was just formality, just the necessary precautions they had to take with a base like Dulce.

There were no other trucks for some reason tonight and Reggie shrugged and didn't think much of it, just turned around the guard station and toward the right-most wall of the huge entry port and kept going, for there really was no way he could hit it, as became clear when his truck started to descend down a concrete ramp set into the floor, one no one could see from the outside of the garage or even in the first work area.

Reggie put his foot to the gas and got moving, now that the theatrics were over. He had a good twenty miles of tunnel driving ahead of him once he made it down the ramp, most just crisscrossing this way and that as he drove deeper into the depths of Mt. Archuleta and the massive underground base it held, all 1,700 paved miles of it, not counting the 800 miles of tunnels that led to Los Alamos.

There was the first level located 200 feet below the surface, where he'd normally check in and out and have lunch. The steel-covered cavern walls were 7 feet high and provided a sense of protection. This area was safe, for humans, and a place Reggie felt the most at ease at while at work, although he could never truly feel fully at ease. He passed the empty work buildings and cafeteria and offices and saw not a person, but kept on, for he remembered what his boss Aaron had said the day before, how today would be different.

A sign up ahead on the concrete walls told Reggie he'd be heading to Level 7 eventually, but he knew that, having been there many times before. It was there that the long trains and shuttles were, the ones that zipped about under the surface of the earth, faster even than the supersonic jets now flying to Paris and London and called Concorde's. It was also here that the large tunnel-boring machines were, the devices the aliens had used to make the massive and worldwide transportation network. There were also maintenance hubs for the UFO crafts that'd helped them ferry the necessary supplies and personal to get them operating.

Reggie pressed the gas and started along. The underground base was massive, more so than even Reggie could probably comprehend, and he didn't mean to dilly-dally – it'd take him a good forty-five minutes of circuitous driving through the ramps to get their. But while his truck might not be moving so quickly, his thoughts were. They continued on, down to Level 3, taking the same round-about and twisting tunnel turns at the end of each level that the truck would be taking soon enough. The ceilings down there rose to 25 feet high when he'd get out into the cavernous highways and turnoffs that led all over place, and then the world. But by staying on the main turnout and ramp he'd have no problems making it the 45 feet to the next level down.

Reggie's thoughts traveled, for there wasn't much else for them to do. No radio was allowed in the base, not even a simple 8-track player. He'd already traveled more than a dozen miles and had barely begun to move past the faceless rows of government offices that rose up on each side of him. The vast amounts of propaganda and misinformation they produced, and where it was directed, he could only guess at, if he ever wanted to. He drove on, again wondering where everyone was at on this day, but again not really wanting to know.

Level 4 would be upon him eventually, and it was here that the research work on humans was done, but it was so much more than that as well. Hypnosis, telepathy, and even the manipulation of dreams were all practiced. Brain chips were implanted in 'subjects' and Delta Waves were used to manipulate the heart rate and brain activity of those they chose. Reggie often shuddered to think of the number of people around the world that were already being manipulated. He was positive he was one.

The buildings rising up on either side of that level's smoothbore tunnels were featureless, and none offered a single piece of evidence as to what they were or what was inside. Reggie had a pretty good guess from what he'd gleaned from other workers, both human and alien. One that always stuck with him were the specially-made rooms made of lead, covered in magnetically-coated steel, and then covered yet again, this time with copper. Such measures were necessary to hold the living aural essences, or souls, of those cosmic beings that didn't require bodies. Reggie also knew that those rooms had been twisted and warped and now did unspeakable things, acts only reserved for God. Sometimes Reggie wondered if God wasn't enslaved somewhere down in the deepest levels, however, the ones even he didn't know existed.

The place was dead at the moment, something he'd never seen before. Glancing down at the odometer, Reggie knew he'd travelled twelve miles already and hadn't seen a soul. Normally he'd be checked and rechecked again before being allowed in here. But not today, and maybe never again.

Level 5 would come after Level 4, and as Reggie steered the truck toward the first curves that would take him to Level 2, he felt a cold come over him as his thoughts raced ahead, one not of temperature but of guilt.

It always came when he thought of Level 4, for beyond it was Level 5, and where the vats were.

He'd never forget the first time he saw them upon rounding the turn and coming onto the level for the first time, rows and rows of them as far as he could see, a forest of them stretching to the far and distant walls of the cavern that was that level. How many humans were there Reggie had no idea, but if he had to guess he'd say thousands, tens of thousands. Although he knew that wasn't quite right – many of the things in those vats couldn't be called human anymore. Many of them never were.

The vats were about 10 feet high and full of amber or green liquid. Most of those closest to the tunnel road were full of human body parts – disembodied arms and legs, the occasional torso and sometimes head, the eyes staring wide and lifelessly out at all passers-by. Reggie tried not to look when he drove through the level, but he always found himself taking a few glances at the vats despite himself. It was what was beyond them that made his hackles rise.

Housed in cages that were perhaps dozens of rows deep were whimpering and crying and screaming humans, and some that were no longer human and that had never been. They cried out for help, for mercy, for death, for their mothers. Reggie had made the mistake one day of having his window rolled partly-down when driving through and had heard some of them, the things they said, the places they were from, their names, their kids' names. He never made that mistake again.

Reggie shook off the thought as he entered the circular ramp that'd take him down to Level 2, the ramp reserved for big vehicles like his, and which took forever to get down at 5 mph. But Reggie's thoughts raced ahead of his vehicle once again, this time to Level 6, Nightmare Hall. The name wasn't a misnomer, either – the place really was the stuff of nightmares. Reggie steered the truck down the curving ramps to Level 2 but imagined instead he was entering Level 6, for he'd always quickly be awash in the pinkish-red light that illuminated the area. And what an area it was! The floors were made of latex and covered with row upon row of cages. If the vats upstairs gave Reggie the chills, these down here damn near gave him a heart attack from fright. He kept his eyes level, straight ahead, never daring to look to his side when he was driving through, even when the Reptilians, the Draco race as they were officially called, had the run of the place.

He still remembered the sight of those…things in the cages. Some had half-human half-animal combinations. There'd been the 'man' with the hands of a seal and the 'legs' as well. A woman that looked more like a unicorn, dogs with human heads, bat-like humans that were 7 feet tall, and things that looked like ten people all stuck together, their faces a mask of bewilderment, pain and anguish. It was the stuff of nightmares, there was no denying it.

The Reptilians were something else entirely. They wore no clothes, just a sort of utility belt that held some of its weapons, and had large claw-like talons on their dinosaur-like feet. What always sent a shiver down Reggie's spine, however, were the yellow, slit-serpentine eyes shining out of those hideous, scaled-bodies. That and the God-awful hissing sound they made when angry. It was they who came to the cages and fed the creatures, and the humans that had yet to be turned into them. And feeding was no easy task. Because of the level of genetic experimentation that'd gone on, several liquid substances needed to be prepared each day, all given out according to the…things' needs.

The proper name for Level 6 was the 'Vivarium,' although what the hell that meant Reggie didn't really have a clue. He remembered when he'd first started at the base, when they'd still been passing the Manual around. It'd described Level 6 as "a private subterranean bio-terminal park, with accommodations for animals, fish, fowl, reptile, and mankind." That was one way of putting it, but there was no way Reggie was ever going to think of cages and tanks as 'accommodations.'

And of course those poor souls were nothing more than chattel, sustenance for the Grays, the dying race that'd started it all, from outer space that is. It began with a few abductions, then the treaties, but when humans proved incapable of giving them all they needed, cattle were turned to. How long those mutilations would be able to be kept quiet was beyond Reggie, but he suspected not much longer. And God did he hope so. The blood of the animals, and that from many of the humans as well, was used to keep the Grays alive, put into the vats where the creatures bathed and soaked up the life essence. The plasma and amniotic fluid were the best, the prime rib of the humans as far as the Grays were concerned. Thankfully they sated themselves on parasitic plants as well, the sap from some even capable of 'powering' them for months.

Reggie shook off the thought and slowed the vehicle as he finally came out of the last of the long and winding ramp from Level 1…and immediately narrowed his eyes.

Is that what I think…sure enough, it was. Three Zeta Reticulan Grays were standing there, the tall grey bastards with big black eyes, no nose to speak of, and that slit mouth that never spoke. Most of the time they were just called 'Ret. Four's,' meaning they were from the fourth planet of the Zeta II Reticuli system, and where the hell that was Reggie had no idea. These ones were a slight shade of green, Reggie noticed, meaning they hadn't 'fed' in awhile, and were more likely to be vicious because of it.

That wasn't really what had Reggie's attention, however. It was the large group of military personnel – the first he'd seen since entering the base – that really threw him. All had weapons, something that wasn't odd but wasn't that common either, and the air in the place had an edge to it, something Reggie could feel even from the safety of his cab. He stopped the vehicle a good hundred yards from the group, who, he now saw, were right near the recently installed antimatter reactor. He rolled down the window of the cab and then crouched down in the seat as best he could, staying out of sight, listening, just like he had in the mud in Vietnam.

Outside in the tunnel a hundred yards away looked to be fifty scientists accompanied by about half as many soldiers. The soldiers all had machine guns while ahead of them the Grays had flash guns. Colonel Michaels saw this and frowned, then stepped forward.

"We're here for the presentation, like you asked. What do—"

"Quiet," one of the Gray's said, or more properly 'sent,' for the word was 'heard' in everyone's mind but not by a single ear. Even Reggie back in the truck a hundred yards away got the message loud and clear.

Colonel Michaels closed his mouth and firmed his jaw and stared into the large black eyes on the Gray's oversized head. He'd long ago gotten over his fear of the things, knowing that they sensed that emotion miles away, like they did all irrational thought. It was keeping the mind rational, logical, but also skipping about in abstract ways that weren't easy to follow telepathically, *that* was the secret to undermining the Gray's dominant hold in all situations with the humans, of which there were increasingly many.

The Gray stared back at him, then sent out the message, "disarm."

"What?" Colonel Michaels said, looking from that leading Gray to its two companions gathered around the antimatter reactor. "What do you mean 'disarm?' We've never had to do that before."

"You'll do it now," another message came, this one seemingly from one of the other Grays, although how Colonel Michaels or any of the others could tell was beyond their ability to explain.

Colonel Michaels shook his head. "I won't."

There was no message this time, just the feeling imparted that that was that, the conversation was over, as was the meeting *and* everyone's life. It was known instantly, as you'd know a breeze was blowing your hair.

Colonel Michaels reacted and managed to get his right hand up, the one holding his machine gun, a fraction of an inch, or about as much as he could in a few fractions of a second. After that the psionic blast from the leading Gray in front of him cut into his forehead and blew his brains out the back of his head as sure as a gunshot at point blank range would. Brain-matter flew all over the soldiers behind him, but they were trained and didn't hesitate as their commander's body began falling to the floor. Neither did the Grays.

Before Colonel Michaels' body was on the floor several more mind blasts came, each blowing the brains out of an unsuspecting soldier. In a matter of moments the floor was littered with a dozen bodies.

For the soldiers' part, they reacted quickly. Machine guns were hoisted and aimed, but trigger fingers suddenly weighed a thousand pounds and wouldn't move.

"Their minds!" one soldier managed to shout out, and a second later his head exploded in an unseen blast.

"Ed…Ed!" another soldier shouted, staring across the few feet that separated him from his nearest companion, Ed Childers, member of Delta Force for more than a year, but now staring with wide and frightened eyes as his arm seemingly moved against his will, pointing the machine gun his companions' way.

"Ed…no!" Ben Dean shouted again, but it was too late. Ed raised the gun up and suddenly his trigger finger wasn't so heavy and was now moving toward its goal, exactly when he didn't want it to. His eyes began to water as his mind revolted against what he was about to do, but his body couldn't object. The machine gun fired to life.

Ben Dean was mowed down as were a dozen soldiers around him. Ed kept firing and crying and trying to say he was sorry but he couldn't stop. The firing continued and then—

BANG!

It was a single shot, but the bullet went right into Ed's forehead and stopped that finger from firing. He fell to the floor dead and Gus Tine gritted his teeth and reached down to grasp the bullet wound in his side, the one he'd just taken from Ed. He'd been lucky enough to survive, unlike many of his companions now lying dead beside him.

"Start shooting, our wounds stopped 'em!" he shouted to the other wounded men around him, just three that looked capable of firing. Of them, two nodded and reached for their weapons, and Gus directed his attention back to the three Grays still standing near the antimatter machine. He took careful aim and—

"Shit!" Chris Evans said as he saw Gus's brains blow out the back of his head, another one of those mind blasts from the aliens. He glanced over at Doug Best, who was the only other one down on the ground with him. Doug had his machine gun up and got a few rounds off, right at one of the Grays and then—

"Shit," Chris muttered again as Doug's brains exploded out of his head. He gritted his teeth, raised his pistol up to his eye, aimed, and fired. The Gray ahead of him – its name was beyond human comprehension – had sensed what Doug was doing, but just a hair too late. The 9mm bullet slammed into the small space between its two black eyes and it jumped back a step involuntarily, then began to fall back slowly. It was dead before it hit the cold steel floor of the tunnel.

A shout went out, but that wasn't quite right, it was more a mental blast of anguish, and it came from the two remaining Grays. They unleashed their fury at the same time they unleashed their reserves. The door behind them that led into one of the many smaller storage chambers opened up and several Reptilians poured forth, each armed with a flash gun.

On the floor Doug was able to smile at his kill before his head exploded like an overripe melon, the mental blast from two Grays hitting him at once. Blood and brains showered those soldiers still around, of which there were few.

The initial firing and mind blasts had taken out more than forty of the scientists and nearly all of the thirty soldiers. The remaining scientists had managed to run back into the tunnels, most heading toward the ramps leading up to Level 1. Some of the soldiers also cut and run, although some were actually pulling back in face of the alien onslaught of mind blasts, trying to protect the fleeing scientists, as was their main duty. Now that Reptilians were pouring forth, and with flash guns, it was a whole new ballgame.

"Run!" a voice shouted, one of the few soldiers still standing near the antimatter reactor, and immediately he became the target of every Reptilian rushing in. It only took one blast from a flash gun and he was vaporized instantly, not a trace of him but a smote of dust that fell to the floor in a barely discernible pile.

That pile was trampled over a moment later by the scaled toe on one of the Reptilians' feet, the large claw-like talons dashing it into oblivion. The thing wore no clothes, just a sort of utility belt that held some of its weapons. Many around it began hitting a small, orange button on those belts, allowing them to vanish instantly from sight. This one simply raised its gun and ran forth, its slit-serpentine eyes shining out as its scaled-body descended upon the mayhem. The creature made a hissing sound and raised its flashgun up, taking aim on another soldier, then firing. The man had been rushing toward the elevator that would lead to the surface, and was vaporized instantly. Several scientists were also rushing that way, and they met the same fate.

In the truck Reggie could hear the scratching and scraping of the Reptilians' feet as they ran through the tunnel, hunting down the fleeing humans. The sounds were getting closer, closer to his truck, and he knew he had to do something. His eyes began to move back and forth in a panic as he thought. *What weapon is there? What can I use? How can I–*

The door to the cab flew open and Reggie bolted up from where he'd been crouching down on the seat, tears of fear coming to his eyes, ready to spill out over that black teardrop tattoo. A Reptilian was there, its broad snout just inches from his face, its yellow and serpentine eyes showing no sign of emotion. In its hand was a flash gun. Reggie's eyes went wide. He managed to open his mouth in an attempt to shout 'no' when the alien fired…and everything went black.

PART I

1 – WAR

Back Alleys – Vientiane, Laos
Monday, December 22, 1975

Turnicot Dupree ran through the rubble-strewn alley and hoped to hell he'd make it to the LZ. *What the hell am I doing this far into the capital, anyways?*

His thoughts were quickly interrupted as a Laotian fighter suddenly sprang out at him from around the next bend. Turn was out of ammo – even though he was still carrying his 9mm – but the soldier didn't know that, and Turn brought the gun up as if to shoot. The move bought him a few precious seconds as the Laotian soldier dove back the way he'd come, no doubt scared to death of the tall black man in front of him. Turn did have scowling eyebrows and a pencil-thin mustache that covered a pair of sneering lips, lips that'd grown up not taking any Mississippi sass, and lips that sure the hell weren't going to take any Asian bullshit.

"Got him!" Turn shouted over his shoulder to his partner Dan, then dashed forward, turned around the corner, and slammed the butt of the 9mm pistol down where he expected the man's head to be, and where it was. The man crumpled to the ground and Turn reached down to—

BOOM!

Turnicot opened his eyes and dust immediately filled them. He closed them again and brought his hands up, rubbing at them for a moment, then opened them again. There was more dust, but at least this time he could keep his eyes open.

"Fuck! Fuck! Fuck!" he said, disappointed in himself, not believing that he could miss the tell-tale sound of an incoming mortar round.

He looked over and saw Dan lying there, clenching his leg, or what was

9

left of it, for it now gone and had blood squirting out everywhere.

"Oh, shit!" Turn said, then began to move over to him. "What the hell just—"

Turn's words were cutoff as bullets ripped into their position, one of them striking Dan right in the forehead and causing his eyes to go wide, then lifeless. Turn's own eyes went wide at the sight, and then he got his head down.

BOOM!

There was a massive explosion and the wall of the building next to Turn seemed to just up and shoot into the air. The last thing Turn remembered was a searing pain in his legs, and then everything went black.

2 – COMING TO

Turnicot opened his eyes and that hazy shade appeared, the one partway between the realm of dreams and the land of the living.

"Who…"

"It's alright, take it easy," a voice said, one Turn hadn't heard before. *It certainly isn't one of the doctors.*

Turn made to nod but then stopped himself and sat still, fluttered his eyes a bit, cajoled the world into making itself known.

"Dan?"

"Dan didn't make it out of Laos. My name's General Harry Anderholt," the man said, closer now – Turn had heard the chair scrape against the floor as he'd dragged it closer, "and I used to be a Major in the Air Force."

"Air Force?" Turn said, his brow furrowing despite the slight pain it caused his head wound.

"What the hell's an Air Force Major doing interested in an 'ol jarhead like you, right?" Anderholt said, jovially, and about the closest he ever came to a smile, although Turn didn't register any of that – his vision was still blurry as hell.

There was a pause, Turn frowned, and the general did the same before pressing on.

"They've no doubt told you by now that your military days are over, haven't they, Turn?" and then quickly, "I hope you don't mind if I call you that…Turn."

Turn shook his head that he didn't.

Anderholt gave another nod that Turn didn't see and then launched into it, like he did with all the other prospects. He knew from experience that it'd only take a minute to tell.

"What if I told you, son, that you could still serve your country, but in a way you'd never believe and could never talk about – would you be

11

interested?"

"Of course."

No hesitation, Anderholt saw. *The first step was passed.*

"The chances that you'd die, even on the very first day, are close to 100% - does that dissuade you?"

Turn's brows furrowed yet again, although most wasn't visible beneath the bandages.

"If I…" a slight pause, "if I was scared of dying I wouldn't a joined up."

Anderholt nodded. "Right." *The second step, complete.*

"Sir," Turn said, and this time he pushed himself up, ever so slightly, but enough, and more than he was thought capable of in his position.

"Go head, soldier."

"I've read a lot of freaky books and seen a lot of wild movies," Turn said, cracking a smile despite himself, "and it sure sounds like what you're getting at here is something, oh…I dunno – out of this world, you get my drift?"

There was a smile on Turn's face, but the general's remained impassive. He held his gaze, locked on Turn's eyes, then finally spoke after several endless moments.

"There's a secret U.S. military base under a mountain range in Dulce, New Mexico," he said, not breaking his gaze at all. "It's been there since 1947 and ever since that date it's been used as a base, staging area, and takeover point for an unknown number of extraterrestrial races. In May of last year the base got away from us, a faction of the aliens rebelled, and we've been locked-out ever since. We've staged over half a dozen missions to retake the base since then, but each of them has failed." The general sighed. "Turn, we want you on one of our next mission…the one that *won't* fail."

General Anderholt still held Turn's gaze and no matter what he did he couldn't break it. Finally five words tumbled from Turn's mouth, five words he hadn't thought about and probably wouldn't have said if he did: "I'd like to help, sir."

Anderholt nodded, rose, and walked to the door. He turned back once more, then gave a slight smile that he had no doubt Turn couldn't see. *Step three, clear.*

3 – WASHINGTON

The Pentagon – Washington, D.C.
Thursday, May 17, 1979

The phone rang. General David Jones gave it a sideways look and kept his pen moving over the paper in front of him. It rang again. He finished his sentence. It rang for a third time, and this time he reached over and picked it up.

"Yeah."

"David," the voice on the other end of the line said.

General Jones sat up and took the phone from under his chin. "Mr. President."

"I want you coming to Vienna with me next month," President Carter said from the other end of the line, "I want you there when we start the SALT II talks."

"But sir…"

"No 'buts' on this one, David – I need you there, I need your expertise."

General Jones bit his lip. *Why now? Why when we're so close?* he thought, but instead said, "of course, Mr. President," nodded a few times after that, then hung up the phone.

He sat back in his chair, the report on aircraft transportation costs forgotten as he stared at the map on the far side of his Pentagon office, the one showing all the major military bases in the United States, and quite a few of the minor ones as well. He stared for a long time, his hands crossed in front of his face, his breath misting upon his knuckles. Finally he picked up the phone, and from memory, dialed the number of one of the few bases *not* on that map, one of the few that even the man who'd just called him didn't know about.

13

~~~

Scott Air Force Base – Illinois

"We've gotta get two placements here and clean up this mess over–"

"General."

General Robert Herres stopped detailing the procurements reports and looked up.

"General, the Chairman of the Joint Chiefs is on the line," Suzy, his secretary, said.

General Herres looked at the junior officer. "I'll get on that and come back later," the young man said, and General Herres nodded, then stood silently over his desk while the man scurried out of the small base office. He nodded at Suzy to close the door, then reached down for the phone.

"Sir."

"The President wants me to go with him to Vienna next month for the SALT II talks," General Jones said over the phone from Washington, "we'll need to move the plans up."

"Move the...," General Herres started, then stopped himself before taking a different tact. "Sir, the teams."

"I know what we discussed and I know what the plan called for," General Jones replied in short, clipped syllables, "but I'm telling you, Robert, things have changed."

"Just because you're going to Europe..."

"With the Russians involved, things heating up in Afghanistan, and the Iranians under new leadership, anything can happen."

General Herres nodded. He'd heard it all before, and they'd been over just this eventuality, well, not quite the SALT II talks, but something pretty similar. They'd all agreed the plan would have to go forward no matter what.

"I know you suffered a serious setback last month when that recon team was discovered," the Chairman continued.

"You could call it that," General Herres scoffed, before quickly adding a 'sir' on the end.

"The original plan called for four combat assault teams," the Chairman continued, ignoring the tone of the junior officer, or putting up with it more aptly, "and we'll have four."

"Four, sir!" General Herres scoffed again, though he'd leveled his tone somewhat – he was talking to the Chairman of the Joint Chiefs of Staff, after all – "with all due respect, sir, where are we going to come up with another team *and* train it in under four weeks?"

"You're going to transition the team leaders you have now and put in some of the new men on each team."

"But sir—"

"You listen to me, general – we don't have a choice in this. That attack four years ago has gone unchecked long enough, we all know that. And we all know the extent to which they've expanded down there in Dulce too, now don't we? So you listen to me, son, and you listen real good – we're going in on the day we planned and the day that moon is right, and we're doing it with four teams. You'll have your new men overnight. Is that clear, general?"

"Yes, sir, it is," General Herres said before swallowing.

And with that the Chairman hung up the phone and the commander of the United States Air Force Communications Command at Scott Air Force Base was left wondering what on earth he'd do.

4 – KIRTLAND AFB

Kirtland Air Force Base – Albuquerque, New Mexico
Friday, May 18, 1979

Brigadier General Harry Anderholt took a sip from his coffee and immediately wished he hadn't.

"*Pttt!*" he spit the coffee out and across his desk, which was thankfully clear this morning.

"I told you it was hot!" Lucille, his secretary, shouted through the cheap wood-paneled walls.

Harry frowned and blew onto the coffee and made to make another sip, then thought better of it and put it down. He was just turning to the back of the sports page when the phone rang. He stared down at it as it rang again, then called out to his secretary.

"Lucille, did a call slip by you?"

"I don't know what to make of that, sir," she called back.

"Don't worry, I'll get it," Harry said, and grabbed the receiver.

"Harry, it's Bob Herres here."

"Bob!" Harry said, a bit louder than he'd have liked, and he immediately cupped his hand over the mouthpiece. "Bob…what the hell?"

"Harry, I've got something big, something I'd like to bring you in on."

"Oh no, Bob," Harry said, already shaking his hand in anticipation of what his sometimes-superior was going to say.

"I need your men, Harry, your special men."

"Not for your mission, Bob, oh no, not for that," Harry said, "I already know they'll be wiped out to a man if you need 'em for what I think you do."

"We can't just let what happened in '75 go unpunished," General Robert Herres said from his paper-strewn desk at Illinois' Scott Air Force Base, "we can't let those Grays get away with this."

"Those aliens should never have been allowed to set up shop here in the first place," Harry laughed.

"Not much we can do about that now, and besides, you had more access to Ike than anyone at the time."

"Not that it did me much good, not on that one."

On the other end of the line General Herres sighed. "Harry, we're moving against Dulce in just a couple weeks. Last month one of our recon teams – six men in all – was discovered and wiped out."

"So abort the mission and start retraining," Harry said, "they should've never have been without alternates in the first place."

"You know as well as I do that this is a need-to-know business we're in here, Harry, and the less that you need to know, the better." Bob sighed again. "Besides, we've got three combat assault teams trained and ready to go, *plus* all our residual forces."

Residual forces, Harry hadn't heard that one. "Like?" he said, his voice rising in anticipation.

"We've got our filter attack team, the one that'll be flying that captured UFO we picked up back in '76. Besides that, it's our material acquisition team, victim assistance team, and of course the clean up team."

"Of course," Harry said, "and so it sounds like you've got all you need."

"No, I need six of your boys, and you'll have them on a plane heading to Blue Lake this evening."

"Blue Lake...what the hell's–"

"Go and see for yourself," General Herres interrupted, "I want you on that plane tonight too, Harry."

"Me," Harry laughed, "what the hell would I be doing going to *Blue Lake*, whatever could possibly be there?"

"Because the Dutchman will be there."

The smile was wiped from Harry's face and seriousness came instantly back to his tone.

"When do you want us to leave?"

"The sooner the better," General Herres said, "the sooner the better."

5 – BLUE LAKE

Blue Lake Secret Hub Base – 70 miles north of Santa Fe, New Mexico

Major Ellis Richards, Jr., known to his equals as 'The Dutchman,' gritted his teeth and got ready to hurl invective.

"God damn it," he shouted, "don't you tell me that we can't get that tracking transponder fixed and back into patrol duty, don't you tell me that for one goddamn minute sitting there with that glum look on your face and that smiley-tart haircut – god damn it, don't you tell me that!"

The Second Lieutenant sitting across the desk from Major Richards had about the reddest face of anyone in a 30-mile radius of the secret Blue Lake naval base, and he shifted uncomfortably in his seat throughout the tirade, managing only a lame 'yes, sir,' when it was finished.

Major Richards chewed his gums and stared from the file folder on his desk to the Second Lieutenant and then back again. Finally he waved his hand in the air and spoke.

"Get the hell out of my sight – and get this mess figured out by Friday!"

The 'yes, sir' had a bit more pep behind it this time, and hung in the air longer than it took the Second Lieutenant to get up out of his chair and out the small base office too. Major Richards shook his head, grabbed the half-smoked cigar from the ashtray, and leaned back in his chair as ht lit it once again to life.

The Dutchman leaned back and enjoyed a puff, the Taos, New Mexico, mountain scenery showing out the window to his back, as well as the deep, blue lake that gave the base its name. His once-brown hair was now mostly grey, but his eyes still had that youthful twinkle and that smile still bedded women half his age, even the ones that knew better. He'd been doing so for more than two decades now, ever since his wife died of breast cancer when she was just 39 and he 42. He looked at her portrait sitting on his bookshelf across the office and gave a self-satisfied smile. Carol would be proud of him, *and* their son Mark, who was now a pilot himself…and a lot more.

Ellis shook his head and scoffed, but smiled despite himself. *Following in the old man's footsteps,* he thought with a laugh as he pictured his son test-flying some of the Air Force's more 'challenging' designs. *Hell, I was the same when I was 32!*

The intercom buzzer rang and a frown quickly replaced the self-satisfied smile that'd taken hold of Major Richards' face, a rare sight indeed.

"Sir," his secretary, Betty, said over the line and from the desk in the outer-office, "there's a…General Herres here to see you and—"

"General!" Major Richards said as he threw open his office door, something he'd rushed out of his chair and around his desk to do, all while Betty was still speaking.

"Major Richards," General Robert Herres replied. He nodded from the other side of the desk with that same confident look that Ellis remembered from their few earlier meetings after the pullout from Saigon. His dark, brown hair was close-cropped yet wavy, and his face sported a perpetual five o'clock shadow. But there were still those creases to the edge of the mouth, giving the hard-faced visage a welcoming look of calm.

"Sir, it's been…"

"Since '75 and Saigon," Anderholt said, finishing the thought for Ellis, and nodding with him, "too long, yet…"

"Not long enough," Ellis finished.

The two men stared at one another, across the miles and across the years and experiences of lifetimes, and didn't need to say a word. They'd had their differences, come to blows once or twice over them in fact, but they did their jobs, still did…always would.

"Betty, can you get us some coffee and also fetch Carl, will you?" Ellis said, still not taking his eyes from Anderholt.

His secretary had seen that look just once before, the one that was reserved for someone she thought of as 'in-the-know,' something she hoped she would never have to be — she knew too much already as far as she was concerned.

She was gone and a moment later Ellis broke off his gaze, pulled up one of the spare chairs in the room, and motioned for General Anderholt to take the other.

"We're going to take it back," Anderholt said as he sat down, smoothing his pants after placing his small, leather travel bag by his side.

"It's been four years, sir…why now?"

"Why not every six months for those past four years?" Anderholt said with a gruff laugh. "That's how often we've tried, on average."

Ellis frowned and bit his cheek. He knew full-well how many missions had been tried and how many had failed – he'd planned and overseen several of the first, and had been 'reassigned,' although that was just a fancy way to say 'saved' from quitting when the frustration of losing team after team proved too much.

"We feel that now's a good time," Anderholt said, leaning forward to put his hand on Ellis' knee, something no other man alive would dare do, but Brigadier General Harry Anderholt wasn't an ordinary man, "and we want you to lead the men, not just from the command station, but from the cockpit."

"Cockpit – hell!" Ellis said, sitting back and laughing. "I haven't flown a crop duster in years, let alone a high-powered test vehicle of some sort."

"Ellis, we want you—"

Anderholt broke-off as Betty came back into view down the hallway, another man close on her heels. Within moments they were in the office, and Ellis rose.

"Carl," he said, grasping onto the man's shoulder and turning him to face Anderholt, "Carl Heinze here chairs the NASA Working Group for the Spacelab Wide-Angle Telescope and also serves as the chairman of the International Astronomical Union Working Group for Space Schmidt Surveys, which as you might well remember, put up the all-reflecting Schmidt telescope earlier this year."

"The one that carries out the deep full-sky surveys using far-ultraviolet wavelengths?" Anderholt said while taking out a pen to chew on thoughtfully.

"Just the one," Carl answered with a smile and a nod. He was a tall man, his brown hair beginning to go gray, but after fifty years, what could you expect? He more than made up for it with that confident look coming from brown eyes that'd seen it all, and then some, eyes that'd most likely be going into space soon aboard NASA's early shuttle test flights.

"That gave us some good information on that mothership that's been around Mercury since 1789," Anderholt pointed out.

Carl nodded again. "Just wait until we get the specs up and running properly and direct them past Proxima Centauri – that's when we'll really get something to talk about."

"Betty, that coffee," Ellis said, and his fazed-secretary scampered off down the hallway once again, this time with the aim of being gone a mighty-long time.

"Carl's the man to put a team together," Ellis said when she was gone, "a flight team, that is."

"That's all I'm asking for," Anderholt said, "a team that knows what we're up against…*and* that can explain it to the men I gather together for you."

"How many this time?"

Anderholt gave Ellis a firm look. "Thirty, including me."

Ellis looked to Carl, and both men swallowed. They'd been on failed missions before, but never been *on* one. Now it seemed even their superior was.

"We're serious this time, boys," Anderholt said as he rose from his chair, "and so am I." He gave them each a firm look. "I'll be back on Monday morning with my men – you better have yours here too."

"Yes, Sir," Ellis said as Anderholt brushed past them and headed down the hall.

The two aged-Air Force commanders stared at one another, all frowns. This was *not* how they envisioned spending their last years before retirement.

6 – COMMANDERS

Blue Lake
Monday, May 21, 1979

"Right this way," the Dutchman said as he held his arm up for Brigadier General Harry Anderholt.

The general nodded and headed into the large room, and Ellis hit the light as he came in after, illuminating the conference room with the large mahogany table and the men seated around it. He walked forward, Carl Heinze close on his heels, though General Anderholt held back.

"Ahem," Carl coughed into his hand, and Ellis turned about, halfway to the table. Seeing the general holding back like that, and the look of doubt on his face, quickly made Ellis reconsider his strategy.

"Let's just skip the pleasantries and get right into it, alright, sir?"

Anderholt nodded and Ellis began.

"Yes, well..." Ellis said, trailing-off a bit before coming back around with a shake of his head. He pointed at the first person at the table, Eddie Okamata.

"Eddie Shoji Okamata," Eddie himself said, taking up some of the slack for Ellis. He smiled and waved at the others gathered, and immediately everyone was set at ease by his presence.

"Japanese?" General Anderholt asked, but Eddie shook his head.

"Hawaiian, born and bred."

"Eddie came up through the University of Colorado at Boulder before getting into the Air Force in '70 and then into the NASA astronaut flight program just last year," Ellis said, and it was apparent looking at the man's thin, black hair, narrow eyes, and smiling face that Eddie had spoken true.

"Air Force, huh?" the general said, giving the younger pilot a gruff once-over, "doin' what...spit-shinin' windows?"

"No," Eddie said with a straight face as he looked off in thought, "just the F-84, F-100, F-105, F-111, EC-121T, T-33, T-39, T-28, and the A-1."

"And the A-7, A-37, T-38, F-4, T-33, and NKC-135," Ellis added before quickly raising his hand to block Eddie's protests. "It's alright – classified has a whole new meaning here, Eddie." He smiled and then looked at the others. "With more than 1,700 test flight hours under his belt, I think he'll do just fine."

General Anderholt harrumphed.

Ellis turned and threw his arm up, showcasing the next man up. "And this is Ronnie McNair, yet another of the just thirty-five men out of 10,000 that NASA chose for their astronaut flight program last year."

"Damn young, ain't he?" General Anderholt said from the corner of the room.

"Just twenty-eight," Ronnie said with a smile that showed off his bright white teeth, a stark contrast to his dark, black skin. He had long mutton-chop sideburns down his face and a mustache that likely killed the ladies, when and *if* he was ever out of the lab.

"A couple of engineering degrees and one for physics and another for lasers thrown in for good measure," Ellis said, "I think we're in good hands."

"And feet," Ronald added with that bright smile once again, "I've got a black belt in karate."

"That'll come in real handy when the Grays are mind-fucking you to death," the general said, something Ronnie could only frown to.

"Next up is Stan Griggs," Ellis continued quickly before Ronnie could get a word in edgewise, "and he's—"

"You don't have to tell me anything about Stan Griggs," General Anderholt said with a smile and a laugh, "test piloted the A-4 Skyhawk, the A-7 Corsair II, and the F-8 Crusader. Turboprops, jets, helicopters, gliders, hot air balloons…hell, I bet Stan there could fly a bathtub if you put wings on 'er."

"Over 9,500 flight hours so far," Stan said modestly from his spot at the table, his lips barely seeming to move from under his large, brown handlebar mustache, "7,800 of 'em in a jet."

The others stared at the quiet NASA astronaut from Oregon, the one many had heard of before. Since '74 he'd been piloting the new space shuttle prototypes and then actual models. Few in the room had as much flying time as he, and that included the many WWII-era craft he collected in his free time.

"Next up is Charlie Beckwith," Ellis said with a 'go-figure' shrug at the general's words, "a man I've known for some time and who single-handedly started Delta Force."

"Chargin' Charlie," Anderholt said with a laugh, "we've all heard his story."

"Well you're about to hear it again," Charlie scoffed, "for I've had to sit through all yours."

Everyone in the room had a laugh at that, and then Ellis continued, regaling them with Charlie's Korean War exploits and then the Rangers School and Special Forces assignments in the late '50s and early '60s. From there it was Vietnam, Laos, and Cambodia, not to mention the classified operations in Thailand and into China.

"It wasn't until '77 that we got Delta Force up and running though," Charlie said at that point, "and that was mainly with the help of the Brits and their Special Air Service forces that were working with hostage rescue at the time."

"It's the best damn force on the face of the planet, bar-none," Ellis said, and everyone nodded to that, even General Anderholt.

"Next is Roger Donlon, and he'll be leading up our final Combat Assault Team, CAT-4," Ellis went on.

Roger nodded at the others, and seemed a bit timid doing so. His blond hair was but about as close as you could get in a butch-cut and he looked just like the all-American boy next door. How anyone could feel threatened by him was beyond them all.

"Call me Donlon," Roger said, "makes it easier for the radio chatter."

"Some of you might remember why Roger here was awarded the Medal of Honor in '65," Ellis continued after smiling. "In '64 he was commanding an outpost at Nam Dong, right on the border with Laos. Two battalions of around 900 men assaulted the small base for five hours, nearly overrunning the 373 soldiers stationed there. Roger was wounded four times but did more than any other that day to hold those forces off. He'll be a fine addition to our team."

Ellis looked over to the general, who only yawned and nodded for him to continue.

"Next up is Aaron Haney, another veteran of Delta Force."

"Don't look it," Charlie said.

"I might only be in my mid-twenties," Aaron said with a smile, "but I can beat your ass into the dirt any day of the week."

Aaron Haney was the kind of guy you wanted on your side in a street fight – skilled, intelligent and disciplined, but distrustful of the motives of some authority figures, especially career-climbing colonels and D.C. bureaucrats. He was a loose cannon in other words, but one that was loyal to his men, and each of them knew it. But that didn't mean Charlie liked his tone.

"Why, I…I don't take that guff from no–"

"Alright, alright!" Ellis said, raising his arms up to stop the two from killing each other right then and there. "You don't have to worry about

Aaron – of the 163 soldiers that tried out for Delta Force two years ago, just twelve made it, and Aaron was one."

"He'll tear your fucking head off, that's for sure," Eddie said with a laugh, and that broke the tension enough for others to laugh a bit too, although just a bit.

Ellis sensed that everyone was growing a bit impatient with the introductions – especially the general – so he hurried it along.

"And last, but certainly not least, is Colonel Stuart Rose."

"Call me Stu," Colonel Rose said with a nod at the others. His red hair was short but wavy and he looked like he probably never did too well with the ladies, but that confident and penetrating look of his showed that beneath those clearheaded, brown eyes laid the mind of a genius.

"Nice white suit there, professor," Aaron said with a laugh.

"Thanks," Stu replied with a smile, and nothing more.

"Stu here started as a smokejumper before getting into the Air Force in the '50s. He was a member of the '66 astronaut class at NASA and then began doing some serious test flights and engineering work, both here and in Japan. He's got 5,500 hours of flight time, nearly all of it in a jet, plus 217 hours in space."

"Space?" Donlon said, a bit taken aback.

"Apollo 14," Stu said, "and I would have commanded Apollo 17 had it not been cancelled in '76."

"Well, we've got a helluva mission for you now," General Anderholt said from the back of the room, then stepped forward. "And now that these introductions are finally over and we know the main men of our team, let's introduce you to our new men, the boys that you'll all be commanding, plus the six…super soldiers."

7 – SUPER SOLDIERS

"Super soldiers?" Charlie scoffed, but he quickly quieted down as a group of men began to filter into the room from the same door Anderholt and Ellis had come through.

"Whoa!" Ronnie laughed. "These boys are…well, just boys!"

It was true – most of the men coming into the room looked barely old enough to shave.

"They're all approaching 30 if they're not past it, and all have seen the battlefield," Anderholt said, his arms crossed over his chest as the men kept coming in, forming a line in the center of the room.

There were many – more than a dozen in fact, and not all of them so young. Many of them actually looked older than the astronauts and specialists sitting at the table.

Finally as the last entered and all nineteen were standing, General Anderholt stepped forward, and Ellis moved over to his side. The men around the table all stood up as well.

"These are the men that'll be heading into Dulce with you," Anderholt said, walking forward to stand in front of their line, "and these six men especially should aid each of your teams. Gentlemen!"

Anderholt stepped out of the way as he gave the command, and six men stepped forward, six that looked just like plain, everyday ordinary soldiers.

"What's so special about them?" Stan laughed.

"Let me tell you," Anderholt said, stepping up to the first man that'd stepped forward, a young man with short black hair that seemed never to have figured out how to lay down properly.

"This is Corporal Tommy Wynn," Anderholt said, "killed in Vietnam in '68."

"What?" Carl shouted, although just a second before Ellis did the same.

Anderholt nodded. "Yep, all six of these men were 'killed' in action,

26

although that's just the official story. In reality, each of them was given a certain amount of telepathic-blocking abilities as well as a special 'gift,' if you will. Tommy's here is to withstand mind attacks.

"Wish I could show it to ya, but I don't think you could see it," Tommy said with a sideways grin, one that showed everyone there that he was a perpetual joker – how else could laugh lines become so deep on one so young?

"Sergeant Sammy Williams here and Corporal Bobbie Baker are the same," Anderholt said, moving down the line to the next two men. Williams was a young black man, clean-shaven and about as clean-cut as you could get. Bobbie Baker, on the other hand, had that mischievous look in his eye that told Ellis right away that he'd be trouble. His hair was cut short and his large ears were prominent, but it was that shit-eater grin that seemed to set him apart. Ellis made a note to bust his balls a bit.

"That's three," Charlie said, "what'd the others do?"

"First Lieutenant Robbie Biscaye here has undergone chemical treatments to make his skin tougher than yours, literally three times tougher."

"Like a rhino," Robbie smiled, his spiky blonde hair sticking up. He had a hard-chiseled face and those far-off James Dean eyes, a pair the ladies probably couldn't resist if they knew he was still alive, which Ellis highly doubted. Nope, it was a good bet none of these six – and possibly the other thirteen – had seen a real woman in years, or at least since shipping off to Vietnam...probably ten years ago now. *How the hell do they look so young?*

"Sergeant Paul Carson is up next," Anderholt said, breaking Ellis's thought, "and he's got one of the most unique gifts – the ability to block all telepathy, not just for himself, but anyone within a 10-foot radius of him."

"Now that *will* come in handy down in Dulce," Carl said.

"Whoa, wait a minute," Charlie said, crossing his arms. "I thought you said they all could do that."

Anderholt shook his head. "Yes and no. Paul here's the only one that can do it all the time, even when he's sleeping. The others, well...let's just say that if you stay within 10 feet of 'em you'll be safe about 80% of the time, how's that?"

Charlie frowned, but held his tongue under the general's intense gaze.

"And the last one?" Ellis asked, already growing impatient with these new 'super soldiers,' although he did see the value they had even despite that last remark by the general.

"This is Turnicot Dupree," the General said, "and his special gift is one most soldiers in the future will have, and that's bionics. Show 'em, Turn."

The soldier named Turnicot nodded and then reached down and started to unbuckle his belt.

"Whoa, there," Ronnie laughed, "I don't know if I need to see no

27

bionics."

"Can it," the General replied, and a moment later Turn had his pants undone and then dropped them to his feet.

"Damn!" Charlie said while beside him Eddie whistled. Before them were two sleek, metal legs, titanium it looked like, although both men suspected it was something much stronger, and perhaps unknown.

"Graphene is what they're made out of," Turn said as everyone marveled at his 'legs,' "one hundred times stronger than steel and a fraction of the weight."

"Those puppies will still be there long after Turn there is gone," Anderholt said.

"Yeah, but will *you* have any puppies here when you're gone?" Tommy said with a laugh and a slap on the back of Bobbie beside him.

Turn frowned, but instead of saying anything just started to lift up his blue and green plaid boxer shorts.

"Well I'll be!" Charlie laughed as the metal legs began to give way to dark, black skin.

"I'd take them up further, but I don't want to show any of you boys up on the *puppy-making* department," Turn said, a sideways look directed Tommy's way. It was a comment that had every man in the room laughing, and even Anderholt cracked a smile.

"And the rest of the men?" Ellis said after the commotion had died down ad Turn had pulled up his pants again.

"The best of the best," Anderholt said as the six 'super soldiers' stepped back into the line and the other thirteen stepped forward. "Each was taken out of active duty while in Vietnam and each has been training with special forces and the new Delta Force since then."

"Those are my men!" Aaron shouted, a second before Charlie was about to do the same.

"But they're *our* tactics," the general said with a gruff look, "and now you'll have a chance to try out your leadership skills with those tactics."

Aaron shrugged at that, and then the introductions began.

"From left to right here we've got Captain Frank Burchak, Sergeant Andy Byrd, Sergeant Billy Brigham, Captain Walter Leathers, Lieutenant Colonel Emil Wiseman, Major Jake Zates, Second Lieutenant David Tish, Major Fred Sayer, Corporal Johnny Williams, Sergeant Lewie Yates, Major John Bingham, Captain Moses Cochrane, and Sergeant Jerry Carol."

The thirteen men stepped back and the nineteen stood there again.

"So you're twenty-nine men, and I'm the thirtieth," General Anderholt said, "this is our team."

The men looked around at one another and nodded. This was their team.

8 – THE GRAYS

Blue Lake
Tuesday, May 22, 1979

The days went by, the men training together, getting to know one another…and learning to put up with one another. They were a disparate group, that was for sure, but a good mix from all the armed forces. And they reflected all the areas of the country as well.

There were the Ivy-League-educated boys, the commanders mainly, though that wasn't really accurate either. While it was true most of the men that'd be flying were from the upper-crust of society, others like Fred Sayer and Chargin' Charlie were not.

Most of the men were poor, or had at least grown up that way. Even though they had money now, most hardly ever used it. They'd give up private lives upon joining the most special of special forces, and few regretted it. Most of the men were white, most from the South. Of the four black men on the team, Sammy and Moses were from the North while Turn was from Mississippi and Johnny was from Georgia. Johnny was just on the reserve team, the one with super soldier Paul Carson and Carl as commander, at least on paper. It was clear to the men after that first week of training together that there were a lot of eventualities, a lot of backup plans, and a lot of second-guessing. But not nearly as much as there was briefings, at least four a day, all so the men could learn what had been hidden from so many of them for so long, the incredible news that aliens not only existed, but were among them, operating by government treaty, and now running amok doing what they willed, something that'd been going on for four years and with consequences unknown and hardly guessed at either, so terrible they seemed.

It was yet another of those briefings, this on a Friday before a weekend

29

that looked to be full of work. The men's morale had never been much lower.

"There are actually several types of Gray," Stan said, continuing on with the now more than hour-long lecture, "it's just that the Zeta Reticuli Grays are the most common, and who we generally refer to when we say the 'Gray.'"

Stan paused and looked out, making sure he had everyone's attention before continuing. He did.

"They're from the Zeta Reticulan star system – the Bernard star – neighboring the Orion area. Zeta Reticuli is nothing more than a dim point of light to us if we're standing outside in an empty area and looking up...though you'd have to be in the southern hemisphere to see it, approximately equidistant between the constellation Orion and the Celestial South Pole."

In the chairs ahead of him, Tommy yawned, audibly and to quite a few grins.

"Not the most interesting at times, I know," Ellis said from the side of the room, "but it just might save your life."

"I find it fascinating," Paul said, and was immediately met with a round of chuckles from the more 'macho' men of the team.

"The Reticulum constellation is relatively close to us, celestially-speaking," Stan continued, pointing at the star map on the wall, "just 40 light years away...or 175,000 years if we were travelling in a regular space craft like we take to the moon."

From the back, someone whistled.

Stan nodded to that. "Of course, that's not practical, so we'd most likely take a craft that could get us there in a fraction of a fraction of the time. But then that's something which we don't have and probably won't for some time."

"At least not publicly," Stu said from the back of the room.

"And that goes with Zeta 2 Reticuli as well," Stan continued, "the name given to the Gray's home world upon its discovery in 1944. Almost immediately it was taken from the list of known and discovered planets, the truth of what it held just too dangerous for the general public to know."

"Despite the Betty and Barney Hill incident in '61," Ellis said from the side of the room.

Tommy again gave an audible yawn.

"So what do we know about these things, sir?" Turn asked, his eyes open and looking on quizzically.

"The Grays function in a mode that's apparently military in nature with a rigidly defined social structure that holds science and 'conquering worlds' to be the prime movers," Stan went on. "Physically, they stand 3 to $3^{1/2}$ feet in height, have a small, thin build and heads much larger than a human's.

There are no auditory lobes, no hair, just limited facial features, a slit mouth and no nose to speak of. Their arms resemble those of a praying mantis in its normal position, and they reach to the creatures' knees, the long hands with the small palm and claw-like fingers of a various number of digits – often two short digits and two long, but some species have three or four fingers. They have small feet with four small claw-like toes, organs that are similar to human organs but which have obviously developed according to a different mutational process. Each has two separate brains, movement that's deliberate, slow and precise. The two separate brains are held apart from one another by a mid-cranial lateral bone, meaning they have an anterior and posterior brain, though there's no apparent connection between the two. Some autopsies have revealed a crystalline network which is thought to have a function in telepathic functions, probably to help maintain the group-consciousness between them. Functions of group consciousness does have a disadvantage in that decisions within the larger Gray collective come rather slowly as the matter at hand filters through the group awareness to those who must make a decision. To top it all off, they've also evolved beyond the need for reproductive systems or digestive systems and now only reproduce by cloning."

"So no kickin' 'em in the balls," Tommy laughed, and a few of the other men joined in, mostly the young and less-educated, like Tommy himself, and Bobbie. They were the two constant jokers of the team, but two they had to put up with – they were super soldiers. Turn couldn't help but think the men's opinion of he and the others was diminished because of the silly antics of those two. But then he knew they were just blowing off steam, getting ready for what lay ahead of them.

"How 'bout kickin' 'em in those big, stupid eyes of theirs instead?" Jerry piped-up next, eliciting another round of laughter.

"Ah, yes...the eyes," Stan said, his voice rising over the rowdy men. "They have large tear-shaped eyes – slanted approximately 35 degrees – which are opaque black with vertical slit-pupils."

Stand paused, as if he were waiting for something, but when it never came, he continued with the lecture.

"These cloning techniques have been given to our government in exchange for 'favors," Stan continued with only a slight frown, like a tired high school teacher that'd heard and seen it all before. "Their genetics are partly based on insectoidal genetics, close relative to the insect family. The larger Grays – known as Type B, or Bellatrax, Grays – apparently have some vestigial reproductive capability, and some of the hybrid species that have been cross-bred with the taller Reptilian species have full reproductive capability."

"Ahem," Ellis coughed from the side of the room, "why don't we get into their minds...if you will."

Stan nodded. "The brain capacity of a Gray is estimated to be between 2500 and 3500 cc, compared to 1300 cc for the average human. Due to the cloning process, the neural matter is artificially-grown brain matter, and the Grays have technology that enables them to insert memory patterns and consciousness into clones in any manner or pattern that they wish."

"Clones?" Charlie echoed.

"Their science deals largely with the study of other life forms and genetic engineering," Stu took up from the back, drawing the men's attention. "They've supposedly had a part to play in the alteration of human genetics over thousands of years. It seems that they may be trying to cross breed with humans in order to create a 'mixture race' that would be better than either. It's commonly believed that they're a dying species, one that's cloned so much that now, with each successive cloning, the species grows weaker. They're trying to infuse new life into their species by creating the mixed breed."

"There seem to be two main social classes," Stan picked up. "One is the more hawkish, more abrupt, crude and blunt. The more dove-like ones are more refined and capable of a business-like behavior towards humans, and prefer to use more 'diplomatic' behavior to gain control over humans. This type of Gray is what I believe is being referred to as the 'Orange' class of Grays."

"So how do we kill the bastards?"

Stan smiled as the men chuckled to Jerry's remark.

"The Grays are photosensitive, meaning any bright light hurts their eyes." Stan paused and waited for the men to get themselves together. "They avoid sunlight, and primarily travel at night for this reason. Camera flashes cause them to back up. That could be used as a weapon against them, but they recover quickly. Still," he continued, giving the men a hard look, "that could buy enough time for an average person to escape. Use commands, or nonsensical words in the form of commands and they will back up. Their brain is more logical than ours and they do not create 'fun'. They don't understand poetry either, so start spouting gibberish if you've got nothing else. What really confuses the hell out of 'em, however, is saying things in Pig Latin. We learned that in a hurry upon our initial infiltrations after the base was lost in '75, and used it against them quite well."

"But not well enough to win," Ellis reminded both Stan and the men.

Stan nodded before continuing. "The Grays read your intent, because they use your body's frequency. The human race broadcasts a frequency, one that they recognize as an electromagnetic impulse. Each person has a slightly different frequency, and that difference is what we call 'personality'. When a human thinks, they broadcast strong impulses, in the case of 'fear' the frequency is 'loud' and easy to recognize."

"And by the same right, a calm and composed mindset should be far more difficult to 'recognize,'" Carl pointed out.

"We can shield ourselves against them, however 95% of the human race never tries to control their thoughts, and controlling our own thoughts is the best weapon," Stan pressed on. "The average person rarely thinks in a clear pattern. That allows the brain to think in a chaotic way. Control your thoughts, and the chances that the Grays can control you – or worse, abduct you – goes way down. Controlling my own thoughts has kept me alive for years."

"You make it sound like bullets won't kill 'em," Turn said.

"Oh, they will," Stan said, "it's just that they'll probably kill a good many of you before you have a chance to make those bullets do any harm."

"That's why these weird mind tricks we're talking about are so important," Ellis said. "I've seen whole teams get wiped out because they didn't try things as simple as that."

"Are their minds really that powerful, sir?" Fred asked, his voice skipping a bit. It was clear he didn't like asking about such.

Stan nodded. "The Grays are primarily situated as 4th density beings, although there are a small number that are 3rd and 6th density. To 3rd density humans they appear cold, cruel and heartless. Nothing could be further from the truth…to a point. They are, in fact, extremely curious about all aspects of existence, highly analytical and devoid of sentimentality. They can experience emotional manifestations radiated from the terrestrial 3rd density human, and use this ability generally as a mood-elevator. The Grays manipulate humans in order to create situations of conflict or extreme pain and emotion to acquire these sensations. They are, in effect, sensation junkies. The Grays have the ability to pick out our emotions, thoughts and experiences. For them, this is the closest they can come to experiencing feeling. Of course to those beings who have some form of ethical conduct – namely, us humans – the Grays appear psychotic and degrading. They are masters of mind-control and mental implantation technique. Their physical attributes reflect their psychotic souls - we could easily consider them to have anti-social attributes as well as tendencies toward megalomania and schizophrenia. They have been described by some as being absolutely mad. To make matters worse, they're performing other actions with terrestrial humans that are quite perverse. The Grays are playing a game with us that depends heavily on maintaining a situation where humans view themselves as limited, fatalistic beings with no control over their own destiny. They continually manipulate humans…that is, they're always playing the domination/control game."

Stan paused there and the men shifted nervously in their seats, like you'd do after something unpleasant or embarrassing had been said. It was clear to all they were up against something the likes of which they'd never seen before, and something that could end them all utterly, and at will.

"What's the security look like?" Carl asked of Ellis, trying to ease the tension that'd suddenly built up in the room.

In response to Carl's question, Ellis nodded at Captain Walter Leathers, who stepped forward.

"There's so much security at Dulce that'd be nearly impossible to cover it all," he said, "and I know this from when I worked down there."

"You were down there?" Billy asked, his mouth slightly open.

Walter nodded. "Was stationed there from '73 to '75 – they pulled me out just a month before the base fell, just dumb luck is all."

"And that dumb luck worked out in our favor," Ellis butted-in. "Walter here was being trained to take over base security before he was sent to inspect the security system of another base. If he hadn't been, there'd be no one alive today that would know what we need to know.

The men nodded at the Dutchman's words, and looked at Walter with some newfound respect.

"The main weapon that the Grays and their Reptilian allies will have besides the flash guns will be a form of sonic."

"Sonic?" Charlie said, shifting uncomfortably in his seat.

"It's built in with each light fixture and most of the cameras, a device that could render a man unconscious in seconds with nothing more than a silent tone. At Dulce there are also still and VCR cameras, eye print, hand print stations, weight monitors, lasers, ELF and EM equipment, heat sensors and motion detectors and quite a few other methods…all using this sonic feature that can kill you at any moment, and with just the push of a button."

"And it's controlled from their main control station, I'll bet," Bobbie said, "so where's that? We'll get in, disable it, boom – problem solved!"

"There's so many types of sensors, radar, infrared, heat sensors, microwave, EMGW, and satellite that I just don't think you'd make it too far," Walter said with a frown, for he wanted what Bobbie had said to work, wanted it desperately, but not so desperately that he'd throw away good men like they were blades of grass in the wind. "Most of the sensors are powered by magnetic power, but the only thing you'll notice on the surface will be an occasional satellite dish."

"What Walter says is true," Ellis said, picking up the tale, "There's no way you could get very far into the base, and even if you *somehow* made it to the second level, you'd be spotted within fifteen feet, your head caved-in like a melon if you weren't just knocked unconscious, only to wake up in some hell called reprogramming that you didn't even know had taken place."

"More than likely you'd just become an inmate and never see the light of the surface world again," Stu added, much to the chagrin of the men present. "If you *were* 'lucky' you'd be re-programmed and become one of the countless spies for the Ruling Caste. At least then you'd get some scraps from the table."

"And if I'm *unlucky*?" Tommy asked, that smirk of his front and center.

Ellis looked over at Walter, who only shrugged before turning back to Tommy.

"Chattel, cattle, maybe some reproductive slave…who knows? Many they use genetic testing on, taking away any kind of humanity as we'd call it, for how do you call some cross between a man and an animal – or two or three – a man anymore?"

"That stuff's down there?" Robbie said, his face twisted up like he was about to be sick at a restaurant and was hurriedly looking for the door.

"I don't know what's down there," Ellis said, "I haven't been there in years – I can't imagine."

There were a lot of deep breaths around the room as men took stock of the situation, and how bad it really was, for their chance of survival, at least.

"So let's say we do make it in," Fred said, looking at Walter, "what then?"

"If we can make it past that first port of entry, then we're really in the clear, as far as what we have to go through."

Walter nodded. "Security is tight at first, but then once we get past it and to the elevators or vehicle ramps, we may well have the run of the place."

"Where's that security command post, the one that could unleash that sonic to kill us with a flash?"

"In the deepest levels, Level 7," Walter said.

"Well then how the hell do we get to that?" Charlie laughed.

"We take the underground train system."

9 – TUBE TRAINS

Whooo wheee!

"Told you so," Walter said with a sideways grin and an equally-sideways look at Charlie, who was now shaking his head after the long, drawn-out whistle of disbelief.

"God damn, the whole planet?" Fred blurted out.

The men were huddled into a small conference room in one of the main Blue Lake base buildings. Before them was a map covering a whole wall, one showing the planet Earth, the regular surface features stripped-away, and a crisscrossing array of what looked to be railroad lines going this way and that in all directions, to all continents and across all oceans.

"They began building it in '54," Colonel Roger Donlon said, drawing many of the men's eyes to him, "got various corporations and government contractors to do most of the work, using the brute labor of the Reptilians to get the job. Project became so big, in fact, that Ike had to get the Interstate Highway System passed in '56 to cover up all the massive spending that was taking place."

"So it's alien-built," Lieutenant Colonel Emil Wiseman said, that ever-present pipe of his clamped firmly between his teeth, even though it wasn't lit at the moment.

"Everything down there is," Donlon continued, "and it's that way in most of the underground bases around the world."

"And most of those bases have been lost to the countries that allowed them in the first place, or built right under their noses while they've sat unawares," Ellis said.

Donlon nodded to his words. "But they don't control the tube trains – not all of them, at least."

"There must be…dozens," Turn said as he continued to stare at the map, "hundreds."

36

"More than 7,600 tunnels by last count, but just forty tube trains to run in them," Donlon said before looking over at Ellis, "unless the aliens have built more."

Ellis shook his head. "We don't think so…but really have no way of knowing."

"So it goes," Donlon sighed. "Anyways, those tunnels are far-from secure, mainly because they can't be secured."

"What do you mean?" Charlie said, his brow furrowed. He'd always been accused of understanding next to nothing when coming up as a child, and he always made it a point to ask and ask away when anyone hinted there might be something he still didn't understand.

"I mean," Donlon continued, "those tube trains are capable of travelling at the astonishing speed of Mach 2. There's no room between those trains and the tunnel walls, so anything walking down them – like quite a few stupid Reptilians or worker Grays often are – they immediately get pulverized."

"Like a bug on my windshield when I'm crusin' down the bayou highways, eh Colonel?" Bobbie laughed.

Donlon frowned. "Something like that."

"And the good news is that after '75 we secured all the tube stations that we could," Ellis said, "which means we now have 75% of them under our control while the aliens just have a handful, mostly here in the southwest."

"It's those ones that we don't have that will be the problem," Donlon said, "and why we need our main force down in those lower-levels, blocking any incoming trains, and the threat to our rear that they could bring."

"So who's gettin' train duty?" Fred laughed.

"You all are," Donlon said, his face straight.

The room erupted in murmurings and buzzing as each man talked to the one next to him.

"Alright, alright!" Ellis shouted over the drone. "CAT-1 and CAT-2 are going to be coming in on those tube trains, and from there you're filtering up the levels toward the surface, destroying as much as you can along the way. On your rear will be CAT-4 led by Colonel Donlon, its sole mission being to block anything else trying to use those trains to get at us from behind."

"So we're not taking the trains out then, right?" Turn asked. He was on CAT-2 headed by Chargin' Charlie and hoped to hell he wouldn't have to come up with an escape plan on the fly.

Ellis shook his head. "Once CAT-3 hits with the X-22 in the hangar port we'll have our opening, allowing both Eddie's Filter Attack Team and Aaron's Clean Up Team to come in and aid you."

"And I'll be flying you out," Captain Moses Cochrane said, the first time many had heard the tall black man with the gaunt face speak up.

The men had turned back in their chairs to get a better look at Command Sergeant Aaron Haney, Cochrane, and the third man on the CUT team, Sergeant Jerry Carol. All were regular Air Force, and looking at them, Turn wondered if they were going to be able to hold their own. They better, he thought.

"What could go wrong?" Carl said with a smile, drawing the men's attention back to the front of the room and the huge map that was there. "What could possibly go wrong?"

10 – AN ASSIGNMENT

"Do they know?" the Dutchman asked as they exited the conference room, he and Carl and General Anderholt taking up the rear. The general had come back just an hour before, on orders from the Chairman of the Joint Chiefs himself, and was pleased with what he'd seen so far...at least that's what Ellis hoped.

Anderholt shook his head. "Not yet, and that job will fall to you men."

"To us?" Carl said, though it was closer to a gasp. "Why us?"

"Half your team already knows, the astronauts," Anderholt said without skipping a beat, "have *them* train 'em."

Carl sighed but Ellis jumped in before the frumpy astronaut could get a word in.

"We'll handle it, sir. We've been training them all week and they're good, not a man is flinching from the responsibility." He paused, then pressed on. "But sir...the men are bored, and unless we send them out soon, well..."

Ellis trailed off as they reached the doors that led back outside, Anderholt's parked Jeep sitting there waiting for him. He spun to face the two men.

"Bored, huh? Well, we'll see how they'll feel after the sortie I send you men on tonight."

"Sortie?" Ellis said. This time it was his words coming out as nearly a gasp.

"In Montana," Anderholt nodded, "a nest of Gray's that's been up there looking at the ICBMs near Malmstrom Air Force Base a little too closely as of late. I want you men to go in and take 'em out before the bastards get it into their big heads to switch off our nukes again."

"But...sir...we..."

"We can handle it," Ellis said with a grin and a hand on Carl's shoulder to stop his stammering.

"Right," Anderholt said, then turned, got into the Jeep, and was soon speeding down the road.

"*Montana*?" Ellis said, turning to Carl as the twenty-seven men of their team headed next door to the larger classroom building of Blue Lake.

Carl shrugged. "Beats the hell out of 'Nam again."

PART II
11 – UNDER THE BIG SKY

Between Lakeport and Hopland, Montana
Tuesday, May 22, 1979

The Aérospatiale SA 330 Puma four-bladed, twin-engined helicopters sailed through the night, their twin-bladed rotors making nary a sound. Inside the ten troops made barely any either.

Ronnie smiled that ivory smile and gave a deep chuckle at Chargin' Charlie's expense.

"What the hell?" he said.

"You look like you got a bur the size of Texas up your ass."

"I don't like helicopters," Charlie replied with a distasteful look, one that caused Ronnie to laugh all the harder.

"Are we really going in to kill...aliens?" Fred said for the third time since the helicopters had taken off from the Blue Lake base.

"Should be a nest of five of 'em," Ronnie said, a bit of his earlier mirth gone, though not all.

"Still don't believe it, huh?" Tommy said, that mischievous smile of his out full force.

"Well...no, no I don't."

Several of the others laughed at that, and even Fred joined in a moment later, his sandy-blonde hair nearly brushing down into his eyes as he finally loosened up.

There were ten of them flying in the single Puma helicopter. Captain Frank Burchak was at the controls and next to him was Sergeant Paul Carson. The other five 'super soldiers' were seated in the back, with Chargin' Charlie, Ronnie, and Fred – the latter being the youngest and least experienced when it came to war, having missed out on Vietnam by just a year.

"How many sorties you been on?" Bobbie said with a laugh. "You sound about as timid as a kitten."

"Well I ain't no damn super soldier like you all, now am I?" Fred shot back.

"Alright…alright," Charlie said, raising his hands to settle Fred down, "take it easy now. Let's save that fight for the Grays."

Fred frowned and held his tongue, but only for a few moments.

"What's the best way to fight those damn things?" he asked.

"Ha!" Robbie laughed. "There ain't no 'best way,' just the only way – hit 'em with everything ya got!"

Fred was getting good at frowning, but even he set a new record when the Puma's red warning lights winked on in the cabin.

"Ten miles out from target," Frank's voice came back at them, "get yourselves ready for insertion."

The men tensed up, even the ones that'd fought Grays before – this was the moment.

12 – LANDING

Turn looked out the Puma helicopter at the dark mountains below.

"Never thought I'd feel safe flying over a mountain," he muttered to himself, then looked over at Ronnie to see if he'd been heard, but the astronaut was engrossed with looking toward where their target should be, some hidden cave nestled in a nook of this section of the Rockies.

Turn frowned and made to do the same, but directed his gaze down to the new 'legs' he had. He still couldn't get over the sight of them, his own 'legs' in their very own uniform. Of course he couldn't get over thinking of them as 'legs' with quotation marks either, and maybe he never would. They weren't those mannequin legs and they weren't those titanium pole legs he'd always worried about getting when he was growing up and thinking of following his father's footsteps into the military, the kind he'd seen on WWII veterans when he'd accompanied the old man to Memorial Day picnics and been regaled with stories of Tuskegee. No, these were something else entirely.

Turn was no confident that he'd never really know what happened in Cambodia, or much of what had happened before. Waking up in that hospital room and seeing an empty bed where his legs should've been was one of the lowest points of his life. The offer of a pair of new ones was one of the highest.

It'd taken months to get them perfectly right, but what Turn most remembered were the first initial days, and it had been days that he'd been worked upon. The tissues at the end of his legs – which now ended well above where his real knees had been – had to be structured with carbon nanotubes, and those in turn had to be propped-up with plant and fungal cells…at least that's what he'd been told. Turn had also come to accept that he didn't really *want* to know exactly how it'd been done.

What he did know was that the legs were state-of-the-art. They had microprocessors that interpreted and analyzed signals from the knee-angle sensors and movement receptors. Any type of motion that Turn made was immediately relayed through the sensors and to his brain, and vice versa. What was truly revolutionary about the cybernetic legs, however, were the hydraulic cylinders in each knee- and ankle-joint. Small valves within those cylinders contained a specially-designed hydraulic fluid, one that did a lot more than just coat the joints that Turn now moved around on…one that increased his speed. And it wasn't any extra second or two in a 100 meter race kind of speed, no, it was more like the kind that'd allow you to finish a 26 km marathon in 15 minutes instead of 5 hours.

They were strong, too. Made with biocompatible titanium that was specially engineered to stay in the body for sixty years instead of the usual twenty, Turn's legs were also alloyed with 4% aluminum and 5% vanadium, the latter giving them about 50% more strength. All in all, it meant he'd have to be hit with a sizeable rocket or run over by a tank for the legs to take much of a dent, although both of those events would most likely kill him before that. That was the thing, Turn thought as he glanced out the window of the Puma – he was still human, and still capable of feeling…even if his legs were not.

"Look alive!" a shout came from the front of the helicopter and Turn quickly looked up to see Frank holding his fist up in the air. "There!"

At the shout, Turn looked out the large bay door and saw a small opening of some kind down below, although it looked a lot more like an old and abandoned mine shaft. Further off there were a few old and rusted derricks sitting on one edge of what could only be called a sizeable-pond, the only other modern feature being a large white cylindrical holding tank of some sort, maybe for natural gas, a crumbling-down shack its only company.

The helicopter circled about, avoiding the large derricks further afield before settling down onto a long corridor where the trees had been cut away, almost as if a landing strip had been laid down. Ronnie immediately began motioning out the large bay door.

"Head toward that cave entrance," he shouted over the sound of the helicopter's rotor blades.

Eight men in the helicopter did so, leaving just Frank and Ronnie behind. Chargin' Charlie was the first out, leading the men with his M240 machine gun raised up high in front of him, and then the super soldiers with Fred thrown in for good measure. Turn looked back to see Ronnie staring at him.

"Go," he said, pointing his drawn gun past Turn and toward the cave entrance, "we'll be back here in 10 minutes – that's all you need for this hole."

Turn nodded, got up and was at the bay door a moment later. He jumped from the helicopter and it immediately began to lift off.

13 – A NEST OF GRAYS

The night was quiet and still and dark as hell. Turn switched on his night vision and quickly picked out the other seven men, all huddled up ahead behind some trees and bushes that fronted the cave. One of them – Robbie by the look of it – waved him over.

"Don't look like much, do it?" Charlie said when he'd drawn near and they were all together.

"Like some dank-ass cave out in the middle of nowhere," Fred replied, two lengthy bullet belts slung over his shoulders and trailing down toward the Colt AR-15 Commando XM177 Assault Carbine in his hands, extras the men had…just in case. Turn looked at him and frowned slightly – neither Fred nor Charlie had ever fought the Grays before…he didn't know how they'd hold up. As if in answer to his thought, Sammy stepped forward, that deep African-American voice of his booming out.

"Just like we briefed on – two teams, side-by-side all the while."

"This cave complex ain't supposed to be much more than half a mile deep, if even that," Bobbie said, spitting a good-sized gob of chewing tobacco down on the forest floor.

Tommy laughed, and Turn had no doubt those crazy eyes of his were darting about under those goggles. "Look at the size of that landing strip – reinforcements could arrive at anytime."

He nodded back behind them and Turn looked to see a straight-on line of nothing, no trees, no bushes, no boulders or anything else that was much higher than a foot. It looked natural enough, but that was probably just because this particular base had been used for centuries, maybe longer.

"Could be coming now, what with all this yappin' we're doin' outside their home," Robbie said.

"He's right," Charlie said, "move out!"

The men broke, just like that, falling into the prearranged teams. Charlie,

46

Turn, Sammy and Tommy took up the left while on the right Fred, Bobbie, Robbie, and the quiet Paul grouped together. They were only fifty yards from the cave entrance, a low-rock overhang on a small hill set before a larger ridge. There were old stumps and moss and rotten limbs piled around, and it seemed as if a mist was in the air just before the yawning maw that was its entrance.

"Corporal," Sammy said, quietly as both teams continued to advance, their guns up and sighted up on the cave entrance, their nerves taut.

"Let's wake 'em up," Tommy said in response, then motioned upward with his arm, although it was more out of habit than any need, "two on either side, near the stumps and logs."

"Got it," Charlie said a moment later, while at the same time Turn said "see it." Both men's guns fired off one of the rocket-propelled grenades mounted on their side and a moment later there were twin explosions about halfway up the hill along the side of the cave entrance where the stumps and the logs had been. Both sent up a shower of sparks, something that'd be unusual if the men didn't know that the sensing and perimeter security guard devices were located there, or at least had been.

"They're onto us now," Bobbie laughed.

"Then keep a lid on it," Fred said over his shoulder. While the six super soldiers may have been the real brains and muscle behind the operation, it was still the two newbies calling the shots.

"I'd keep a lid on it if you weren't so—"

Whatever insult Robbie was about to hurl Bobbie's way was cutoff as a large turbine-like sound started from the cave entrance, or at least somewhere within, and quickly grew in pitch and frequency and volume, until the lights burst on.

"Shit!" Charlie said up ahead, then ripped the night vision goggles from his head at the same moment everyone of the other med did the same.

"Down!" Fred shouted next, gaining a bit of his senses back, and right as he dove down to the brush beside him. It was a good thing, too, for at just that moment some kind of rocket or something shot out and exploded right near where he'd been.

The others did the same, and the rockets – there were actually four shooting forth – all landed where the men had been or had been going. Still, the men had been far enough away that they were only showered with dirt and branches and leaves as the missiles impacted upon the forest floor. And that's when Turn saw them.

"There!" he shouted, putting his arm up while pushing his M240 machine gun up with the other, getting it up over the small dirt mound and pointing at the Gray right there at the cave entrance, just inside, the earthen walls illuminated now by the floodlights shooting outward, blindingly so, but not so blindingly that Turn couldn't see the thing's face, and what he hoped was fear in its eyes.

"Light 'em up!" Charlie said, and a moment later the men did so.

Turn was the first to get a shot off, or at least he liked to think he was. The Gray he'd pointed out was in his sights and he pulled the trigger and saw the bullet hole appear in its head. Greenish-ooze began to seep out – not blood, Turn knew, but that vat liquid they used below Dulce – and the thing fell forward.

A shudder went through Turn's body. He'd killed them before, but he never got over how strange it was, how…different. When you killed a man you could see his eyes roll up or flutter shut or just the life go out of them. When you killed a Gray…nothing.

Sometimes he didn't think they were dead, for there was never any expression in those faces, never any 'humanity' in those black orbs they called eyes. But they were dead, he knew, and that was what made all the difference, and why he'd know they'd win eventually, because they *could* be killed.

"Look alive!" Sammy shouted ahead of him, knocking Turn from his thoughts. He blinked a few times and focused his attention back on the cave entrance, and was surprised by what he saw.

"They're on the run!" Tommy shouted in glee from beside him.

It was true – there were just three dead Grays in the mouth of the cave and the lights were beginning to dim, although they weren't going out completely.

"Into the rabbit hole, boys," Charlie said with a laugh, and once again Turn admired him for his bravery, his courage, and his blind-stupidity. The men did as well, for they gave a 'hell-yeah' and started forward.

Fred's group was moving ahead slightly faster than Charlie's, mainly because Bobbie kept jumping up ahead, his enthusiasm to kill the aliens outweighing his sense of safety. Fred was able to hold him back, but they were getting out of formation because of it.

"Pick it up," Sammy said, and he pushed forward ahead of Charlie.

Charlie didn't protest, and a few moments later the men were at the cave entrance, the dead Grays at their feet, the lit-tunnel open before them. The mouth only went a dozen feet before hitting the back wall, although the tunnel itself twisted to the right. They reached that turn and started around it.

"Damn!" Sammy shouted, then fired three short bursts. The Gray that'd appeared ahead of them fell to the floor, followed a moment later by its head, shot off at the neck."

"Whoo-ee!" Bobbie laughed, then whistled too for good measure. "Love it when that happens!"

Charlie and Fred gave him a strange look as they reached the creature, and got their first real good look at the things they'd only until that point heard about.

"Damn those eyes are lifeless," Fred said, and Charlie nodded.

"So's their souls," Paul said, the first words out of him since they'd gotten off the helicopter.

"Why the hell'd that one just stand there and let itself get shot to shit like that?" Charlie said, his mouth hanging open in surprise and his eyes darting from one super soldier to the other.

"Thought he could get me," Sammy replied, looking at the two 'commanders' of the mission.

"He didn't know that Sammy, Bobbie and me ain't susceptible to that mind attack crap," Tommy said, in a serious tone for a change.

"That's why you all need to stay close to us," Sammy said, looking at the others but especially at Charlie and Fred. "Stay close to us and you'll be fine."

The men nodded and they started forward again. The lights were still on, some kind of dull-yellow orbs built into the side of the tunnel, which was now beginning to turn to metal, the walls at least.

"How far's this thing go down?" Robbie asked no one in particular as they kept on moving.

"It's a shuttle port," Paul replied, "could go on for miles."

"You said a half mile outside there," Charlie said, turning to Paul.

Paul shrugged. "It's hard to say, though the intel on this one said—"

"Shut up!" Turn said as loudly as he could without shouting. "Listen."

The others listened, then the super soldiers looked at one another and their eyes went wide.

"Get down!" they shouted as one, then dove for the sides of the tunnel. Fred and Charlie did the same, their training taking over for any lack of understanding, and a moment later a 'whooshing' sound of some sort could be heard.

"Robbie!" Sammy yelled at the same moment some kind of UFO flew over their heads.

"Got it!" Robbie shouted back, and he did, his M203 China Lake model grenade launcher pointing forward and ready. He hit the button and the thing fired to life, shooting out after the UFO as it was just reaching the turn to the tunnel entrance.

"It's not gonna—"

BOOM!

The missile-like grenade hit the side of the tunnel entrance just as the UFO darted to shoot out of it, cutting-off Tommy's words. The missile missed, but the rocks that flew out and the other shrapnel didn't, and the men all clearly saw the thing shudder and flinch and look like it would crash...but it didn't.

"C'mon!" Turn shouted, rising up faster than the others with the help of his cybernetic legs.

He was also able to dash down the tunnel before his companions were able to take a few strides. The legs allowed him to reach the tunnel entrance to see the UFO shoot out down the landing strip the Grays had for it, then upwards…and right toward Frank and Ronnie coming back in the Puma!

Not that it mattered, he quickly saw, for the UFO was still shuddering and now shaking and about to drop at any moment. It gave a valiant effort trying to pull itself up toward the helicopter – which was over the treeline and still a hundred yards further on, Turn now saw – but it failed miserably. All at once the lift seemed to give out of the craft and it dropped to it's right, the same side that'd been damaged in the tunnel blast, and then clipped into the tall Douglas Fir trees that were standing there. The sides dented and sparks and smoke flew out from the spaceship, but it didn't blow and it didn't disintegrate. Instead it fell to earth and landed with a resounding crash, something that could probably be heard for miles.

"Damn!" Fred said, and Turn looked over to see him there, panting from the run down the tunnel. He looked back and saw the others would be there in another few moments.

"Looks like that shot of yours did it!" Turn yelled, and just as Robbie reached them. He raised his arm up and pointed toward the trees where there was a small plume of smoke rising and nothing more.

"Well I'll be damned!" Tommy shouted. "I thought for sure you were gonna keep up that near-perfect record for misses."

Bobbie spat out a large wad of tobacco. "Like you're trying to keep that perfect record of not getting' laid?"

"Alright, alright!" Fred said with a laugh. "Let's get out there and give those boys a hand."

He pointed toward the helicopter, which was beginning to land a short distance from the crashed UFO, though still on the landing strip.

"What about the tunnel," Paul said, stopping them all as they were about to rush forth, "what if there are more?"

"He's right," Charlie said, then looked to Fred, "you and your boys stay here and head back down that tunnel a ways, see if there's anything there."

Fred frowned, but nodded – he didn't want to miss out on the action, but he didn't want an unnecessary risk at their backs either. He'd seen enough of what unguarded tunnels had done to his platoon of men back in 'Nam.

The others headed toward the helicopter, Sammy leading the way again with Turn and Tommy and Charlie close together. They put their night vision goggles back on and ahead of them saw that Captain Frank Burchak was getting out of the helicopter's passenger seat. He waved at them, then looked over at the crash site, got the rest of the way out of the craft, and began to close the door.

"What's he doing?" Tommy said, shock in his voice, his tone serious. "What the hell is he doin' gettin' out there alone!"

"C'mon!" Sammy shouted, then started to run forward more quickly.

It was too late. Frank was walking forward and had just about cleared the helicopter when he jerked to a stop, as if some invisible hand had suddenly grabbed him. Even with the night vision it was clear, the look of terror on his face. He had no control over his arms or legs, but his face took on a twisted look of terror as his body slowly began to rise off the ground.

Inside the helicopter Ronnie sensed what was happening and flipped off the helicopter's rotors, but he knew it was a futile effort as soon as it was done. Ahead of him Frank's body spun around so his face was looking straight into Ronnie's, the look of terror evident, his eyes pleading for some kind of help that could never come but which his mind wouldn't let him believe.

He screamed, but it was a short burst of sound before his head turned back against its will and his body shot upward face-first into the spinning rotor blades, still moving at more than 500 feet per second. Blood drenched the helicopter's window and all Ronnie could see was a curtain of blood.

Turn gritted his teeth. "C'mon!" he shouted, then took off, his cybernetic legs carrying him the hundred yards to the helicopter in just seconds.

"Shit,' Sammy said as he and the others began running, hoping to get there in twenty seconds, and before the Grays still alive in that crashed UFO could do the same to Ronnie as they'd just done to Frank.

Turn reached the spot where Frank's body lay, the head and face gone down almost to the neck. He narrowed his eyes and focused on the spot where the UFO had crashed.

There! He saw it in his night vision, two forms moving–

He couldn't move, his limbs were stone and ice and locked in position. He felt a tingly sensation, then his feet left the ground. *Guess that 20% finally caught up with me*, he thought.

"Not so fast!" Tommy shouted, picking up his pace and running as fast as he could. It was fast enough, and when he was within ten feet and Turn was within inches of the rotors, the power of the alien's telepathy attacks faded altogether.

"Three!" Turn shouted, his voice now back, for he'd been trying to shout all the while that there was another alien, he was sure of it, for no Gray he'd ever heard of could use that much mental energy while rushing away as fast as those two he'd spotted had been.

"Fire in the hole," Charlie said matter-of-factly, then pulled the trigger on his grenade launcher twice in quick succession. There were two 'thwumps' back to back, and then a moment later twin explosions in the trees where the two Grays Turn spotted had been running.

"Where's the other one?" Sammy yelled.

"There," Turn said, locking onto it, and raising his gun up to nearly point at the men that'd rushed up to save him. They jumped out of the way and Turn fired three quick bursts from his machine gun, then looked where he'd fired to see a Gray's head explode in a shower of 'blood' and brains near the cave entrance.

Turn lowered his still-smoking gun and looked at his companions, many on the ground from jumping out of the way.

"Fucker," he spat, and the men began to laugh.

14 - DEBRIEFING

"Well men – that nest of Grays is cleaned out!"

There were only nods to Ellis' words, for the men were tired and what's more, the realization that they'd lost one of their own was finally beginning to sink in.

All around them the teams from Blue Lake were moving about, more than two dozen men now. There was Eddie and Stan helping with the crashed UFO, and Stu doing mop-up work inside the tunnel to see what technology and information could be gleaned.

Fred and his team had come back just minutes after Turn had shot that third Gray from the UFO outside the tunnel entrance. They'd reported that there'd been no more Grays, but quite a bit of equipment, testing areas, and most surprisingly, a few vats.

"Those were just supposed to be at Dulce," Ellis had said upon first hearing the news shortly after his arrival and initial debriefing of the men.

"There was supposed to be a lot of things," Carl had replied to him, "but '75 kind of changed all that."

Ellis didn't like to hear that, but then he often didn't like to hear the truth. He *needed* to hear it, though, and in this case the astronaut was right.

"Listen," Ellis said, a frown coming to his face, "you men have done a good job tonight, a rough job, but one that needed to be done. Now let's get you back on that chopper and back to base."

The men nodded and were soon filing into the Puma a short distance away, a different one than had been drenched in Frank's blood.

"Well, what'dya think?" Carl said to Ellis when the men had gone and they were alone in small army of military personnel, scientific geniuses and quite a few crack – and crack-shot – researchers.

Ellis took in a deep breath. "I think we need these men storming Dulce, and as soon as possible."

"You're not worried they're not ready, especially the ones that didn't go tonight?"

"They're ready," Ellis said, turning to look at the helicopter as it rose up into the air and then started over the tree line to be swallowed from sight, "the question is, how ready for them are the Grays?"

"Not to mention the Reptilians as well."

"Don't remind me," Ellis groaned, "if they've managed to multiply as much as we—"

"Commander!"

Both Ellis and Carl spun around to face the cave once again, and saw Stu rushing up to them, his usual white lab coat fluttering behind him as he ran.

"We've found something," he said when he'd reached them, "we've found something big."

"Big as in size or big as—"

"Both," Stu said, "and in a few different ways – why don't you both come back inside the cave…although we really should stop thinking of it that way."

"Oh?" Carl said. "How should we be thinking about it?"

"Perhaps as a shipping port."

15 – DISCOVERIES

Ellis and Carl followed Stu down the last of the tunnel, past the area where the men had dodged out of the way of the UFO, and then around the next bend and to the hangar, for that's all you could really describe it as.

"Damn it's big," Ellis said when they got to the entrance, "how the hell'd they build this right under our noses?"

"They seem to be doing a lot of things right under our noses," Stu said, "come on – let me show you."

The two men had little choice as the astronaut and scientist started forward, into the hangar. It was a good forty feet to the ceiling and nearly a hundred yards from one wall to the next as they walked through the center of the thing.

"It only goes fifty yards further into the mountain," Stu said as they walked past what looked to be marked-off 'parking spots, was all Ellis could think of them as, each totally made up of strips of lights embedded into the metal floor.

"What's that door up ahead lead to?" Carl asked, pointing at the only real features on the far wall, now just a couple dozen yards ahead of them.

"It's not a door, not like any kind we know or saw at Dulce," Stu replied, "but it does lead somewhere."

"Where?" Ellis said.

Stu walked on the last few yards without saying anything, and then they were at the door, and he turned to them and smiled.

"The real hangar, that's what it leads to."

~~~

"Holy…"

"Yeah, that's what I thought when I first saw it," Stu smiled, looking

55

from the craft to Ellis and back again, "we figure it's more than 100,000 square feet."

Ellis didn't doubt it, not for one second. The huge UFO mothership – *what else could it be?* – was at least the size of three football fields in length and probably three-quarters of one in width. It was a serious ship, meant to travel between galaxies, but also meant to hold a lot. Beside him, Carl seemed to have read his mind.

"What are they transporting in it – have you been inside?"

Stu nodded. "My team just got it open, I went in, and that's when I came running out to you."

"What is–"

Stu raised his hand, cutting-off Ellis's words.

"Just come."

~ ~ ~

Stu hit the button beside the door and the two double-doors slid open. Ellis and Carl's eyes went wide. There before them were row upon row of vats, all aligned orderly, and each holding...something.

"What's in there?" Ellis said. "Please Stu, don't tell me that's what I think it is."

"It is," the astronaut replied, "they've broken all aspects of the treaty."

Ellis agreed and would have nodded had he not been in so much shock. There before him were the large glass vats he'd first seen deep down on Levels 5 and 6 of Dulce the last time he'd been there, in '75, the dreaded Hall of Horrors and Nightmare Hall. Inside they held human body parts, organs and fluids. There were also cow parts, from the many farm mutilations that happened each year, most of which went unreported. The Grays needed the stuff, needed the human and animal essences to live, to continue their race.

The Grays didn't eat, but instead 'fed' off of human and animal vital fluids by rubbing a kind of 'liquid protein' formula or slurry onto their bodies, which was then absorbed through the skin. This biological slurry mixture was mixed with hydrogen peroxide, something that oxygenated the slurry and eliminated bacteria. Like reptiles which shed their skins, this 'waste' was typically excreted back through the skin. It was those skin excretions which were responsible for the different color hues the Grays sometimes took on, which ranged from gray-white to grey-brown to gray-green to grey-blue. Aside from feeding off human and animal proteins and fluids, they also allegedly fed off the 'life energy,' the 'vital essence' or 'soul energy' of humans, as did other Reptilian species...like it was some kind of recreational drug, almost. And when a human has had that energy and essence taken from them – like many of the humans no doubt imprisoned in Dulce at that very moment had – then they appeared as programmed 'drones,' 'lifeless' and 'emotionless' to those that observed them.

It was those subsistence methods that really rubbed humans the wrong way, however. They required human blood and other biological substances to survive, although every indication suggested that they originally didn't 'require' human blood, but once having used it they since acquired a taste for it, if you will, and considered it a 'vital' substance. This went far beyond just mere physical hunger, since the Grays tended to feed off the human life-energies resident within human blood plasma, in what may be considered a vampire-like type of hunger for human vital fluids. In extreme circumstances they could subsist on other, animal fluids...namely cattle.

The Grays were the ones involved in the cattle mutilations, absorbing certain substances from parts of the animals, parts that stabilized them during the cloning process. These substances could then be placed under the tongue to give sustenance and stability for some time. It's a substance that came from certain mucus membranes, such as the lips, nose, genitals, rectum and other organs, so there's always more.

The Grays were beginning to stockpile canisters and vats in which animal and human organs floated, along with a greenish-liquid to hold the parts in suspension. The Grays swam in the mixture, absorbing the nutrients through their skin. But those tanks were few in number, and all in Dulce. Now the three men were standing and staring at row upon row of them, each filled with human and animal parts, yet not a single one holding a living creature.

"How many do you think there are?" Carl asked after they'd stood there in silence for a few moments, just staring out at the ungodly sight and thinking upon the Grays and their insidious ways.

"Hundreds, maybe thousands," Stu said. "This is obviously some kind of transport ship or ferry, one I've no doubt is intended to supply the larger mothership stationed around Mercury."

"So their numbers are increasing then," Ellis said, looking over at Stu for some kind of confirmation. The astronaut and physicist nodded, and Ellis shook his head. "Damn it – it wasn't supposed to be like this! When Ike signed that treaty in '53 it was supposed to be a few abductions, a few tests, just what they needed to stay alive."

"It won't be the first time a president was lied to," Carl said beside him.

"I figure it had to have started after the incident in '75," Stu said, speaking quickly before the obvious frustration Ellis was feeling could manifest itself in harsh words. "After that they probably figured the cat was out of the bag, at least in regard to U.S-Gray relations, and they notched-up their harvesting."

"Harvesting," Carl scoffed, "that's one way to put it!"

"I'd rather use that term than describe the process of stealing these women's innocence, robbing them of their humanity, and turning them into some other life form entirely…and don't think for a second that women aren't being used more than men now."

"How do you know?' Ellis asked. It was well-known even back in the '50s that the Grays were experimenting on women a lot more than men, but had that increased further?

"Let's just call it a hunch for now," Stu said, "but one that I think I'll be able to prove shortly…that is if you let me into Dulce."

"Whoa, Stu!" Ellis said. "You know full-well we need your expertise here on the surface."

"And out of danger's way," Carl added.

"You need me in that base," Stu protested as he shook his head and crossed his arms in front of himself. "You have no idea what could be down there, no idea what kind of weaponry or gadgets or technology could kill you in flash, or aid you beyond your wildest beliefs."

"I hear Carter's looking for a new speech writer," Carl said, looking over at Ellis.

"Oh, c'mon!" Stu nearly shouted, and both Ellis and Carl fell into laughter.

"Alright, Stu," Ellis finally said when he'd pulled himself together, "we'll let you in – but on one condition!"

"Which is?"

"That you don't come in until the top level is secured."

"And the lower levels as well," Carl added, and Ellis nodded.

"The lower levels," Stu did shout this time, "you've got to be kidding! How are you going to secure those lower levels?"

"We're working on a plan now," Ellis said while giving a frown to Carl.

"And we're not getting too far on it standing here and flapping our gums," Carl replied. "Let's get back to Blue Lake and leave you here, Stu, to reverse-engineer this sucker."

Stu smiled for the first time that day. "Oh, now *that's* something I've been looking forward to!"

16 – DRAWING LINES

Blue Lake
Wednesday, May 23, 1979

"What the hell just happened back there?"

Turn slammed his helmet down on the floor and it bounced against the opposite wall, the steel clanging around the room.

"Take it easy," Robbie said, "we just got hit by the Psy's, that's all."

"The...'Psy's'?"

Across the room Tommy shook his head and muttered something under his breath, and that just made Turn want to punch someone's lights out even more. David must have noticed this, for he spoke up.

"He means Psychics," he said, giving Tommy a nasty glare, although that just resulted in the hard-headed soldier smacking his hand into his fist and looking tough. David brushed it off with a scoff and looked back to Turn. "They've wiped out hundreds of us that way...maybe thousands."

"*Thousands?*" Turn said quietly.

"Oh, don't be all melodramatic," Robbie said with a laugh. "Turn, they're not as dangerous or as powerful as you might believe, they'd want you to believe, or," he looked around a bit and then lowered his voice before pointing up toward the surface, "*they'd* want you to believe."

"Don't give me that horseshit," Tommy said, pounding his bunk for good measure, something that caused it to skitter across the hard concrete floor a bit, "if those aliens wanted to wipe us out they could, any moment, any way."

"Then why aren't we dead?" David said.

Tommy scoffed. "They're toyin' with us."

"Yeah, *toyin'* with us," Robbie mocked, "and I guess that's why we just wiped out a whole nest of 'em in Montana and plan to wipe out a base worth here in New Mexico, huh?"

"A nest?" Turn laughed. "Give me a break – we killed seven Grays, nothing more than a drop in the bucket."

"Drop in the…I'm sorry, but can someone please explain what Turn means?"

Tommy looked over at Fred and shook his head then laughed.

"Ah, hell," he said, "I'll explain it, but I can guarantee you're not going to like it."

Fred nodded.

"Alright, here goes. The Grays abduct humans and animals in order to acquire the bodily fluids they need to survive. They implant small devices near the brain which potentially gives them total control and monitoring capability, ensuring once a host is taken, it can always be taken again."

"Like collaring a dog," Robbie laughed.

"These devices are very difficult to detect," Tommy continued. "When we've analyzed the devices the best our experts have been able to come up with is that they use some sort of crystalline technology combined with molecular circuitry, and together these ride on the resonant emissions of the brain and the various fields of the human in question. Information is entrained on the brain waves and each and every time we've attempted to remove the implants it's resulted in the death of the human that we're trying to save."

"This is usually due in part to the fact that the implants are attached to major nerve centers, and once attached the nerve tissues grow in and around the implant essentially making the implant a part of the nervous system," David said, standing up for a moment. "When relatively unsophisticated medical procedures are used in an attempt to remove the implants, major nerve centers are damaged as a result, causing severe injury or even death.

"Who do they take most?" Fred asked.

"I can tell you that the most common abductees are petite women in their early twenties or early thirties, dark haired boys between five to nine, small to medium size men in their mid-twenties to mid-forties," Jerry said with a sigh from across the room, as if he was saying something he'd rather not. "But, let me stress that there are all types of people being held against their will in the Dulce Base! There are tall heavy men and women, teenagers, elderly folks and very young girls in the cages and the vats. I only mention the most common age-size are the small young men and petite women. The boys are favored because at that age their bodies are rapidly growing, and their atomic material is adaptable in the transfer chamber. The young small women are frequently very fertile. The men are used for sperm. I have no idea why they prefer small to average size men."

Fred's face lost a bit of color. "Jesus!"

"Yeah, but don't you think it's funny that none of the briefings we had over the past week or so have mentioned why the Grays are here, why they broke that treaty, and why we need to get back into that base so bad?" Lewie said from across the room.

"You know why," Tommy said, looking over at him with narrowed eyes and in the calmest voice Turn had heard him use yet.

"Don't be—"

Lewie was cutoff as Carl suddenly strolled into the room.

"Listen up, men," he said, coming to a rest just inside the door, his hands behind his back, and seemingly oblivious to what they'd just been talking about, or at least acting that way, "we've got new orders already."

"What?" David nearly shouted. "How could that—"

Carl raised his arm and David fell quiet.

"After that attack last night we're not taking any chances and we're not letting them change up their defensive or offensive capability – we're going in."

He looked over and gave Tommy a stern look, but the hard-headed soldier wisely held his tongue. Carl glanced around the room at the others, nodded, then turned to leave. "Be ready to move soon," he said, then was gone.

17 – DIFFERENT VIEWS

Blue Lake
Thursday, May 24, 1979

Turn rushed to the door in the white storage tank, the gravel crunching under the heels of his boots. He reached it faster than he'd ever run before, and it surprised him. He often had no idea his legs could do what they could, but he wasn't going to gloat over it now – he whipped his hand down and grasped the doorknob and turned and...nothing – it was locked.

"Shit!" he said, then looked back over his shoulder. It was then that the flash gun hit him and he vaporized into a fine black powder, one that started to blow away on the wind.

BEEP!

The buzzer sounded, indicating the simulation was over, and a moment later the virtual reality goggles lifted off Turn's head.

"Second time," the soldier manning the sim-chamber said as he set the goggles down on the table next to the dentist's chair Turn was sitting in – it was technically called the V-Chair, but technicalities didn't usually fly too well at Blue Lake.

"What the hell was that?" Turn said, then looked up at the man standing over him. He wasn't wearing any kind of military uniform, and in fact had on an oil-stained wife-beater and pants that didn't look much better – *was that blood?*

"That, my friend, is a common problem we get at the HUB drop-off points," the main said, then stuck his hand out in a gesture to help Turn up. "Name's Zates, Major Jake Zates...I don't think we've met yet...at least besides that initial meet and greet..."

"Which wasn't really much of either," Turn said, then smiled and put out his hand.

"Turnicot Dupree," he said, then screwed up his face. "Zates? Sounds…hey, what kind of name is that, anyways."

"Beats the fuck out of me," Jake said, "maybe Pollack – I dunno. What the hell kind of name is Dupree?"

Turn laughed. "Cajun, what else?"

"Louisiana boy, huh?" Jake said with his best New Orleans Cajun accent, which was close-up to the worst Turn had ever heard.

"Mississippi," he said, smiling nonetheless, then narrowed his eyes and became serious. "I thought I was on a military base in that sim? What the hell was that back there?"

"Oh, you've probably thought a lot and made up a lot of assumptions on where you're going," Jake laughed, "but let's just clear all that rubbish away now, eh?"

Turn frowned and was about to speak up when another voice beat him to it.

"Don't scare him, Zates – not yet at least."

Both Jake and Turn whipped around to see the Dutchman standing there.

"Ah…Major," Jake said, then nodded deferentially as Ellis approached.

"I'm glad to see you're training," Ellis said as he came near, ignoring Jake completely but stopping beside him, "I wish more of the men felt the need."

"Where we're going?" Turn scoffed. "I don't see why they don't."

Ellis frowned, glanced over at Jake, then nodded. "Not that it really matters – we'll be heading out tonight."

"What!" Turn said, nearly bolting up from the chair even though Jake was still working on the last of the connections to him.

Ellis nodded. "We've got word that an alien transport ship is coming into the Dulce port tonight, one that'll ensure the port is open to us, and one that'll give us some extra cover to boot."

"That's *one* way of putting it," Jake said with quite the audible sigh, "another way is to say the Grays will have more…'men' in that port area than they'd usually."

"You sound like you know a lot about the aliens, Jake," Turn said, "I thought most of you regular recruits were in the dark. Well," he said with a laugh, "at least until I heard some of you talking last night – what the hell is going on with you boys?"

Jake gave a nervous glance to Ellis, and the Dutchman nodded before putting his hand on Jake's shoulder.

"You know that not every mission we sent into Dulce had a 100% casualty rate, right, Turn?"

Turn looked to Jake, who's eyes flitted about nervously, like he was picturing something he'd rather not see. Turn nodded, said nothing.

"Now Jake here," Ellis said as he tousled the young man's hair, breaking a bit of the tension, "Jake here was working in Dulce *before* '75."

"*Really?*" Turn said, narrowing his eyes at the young soldier.

Jake nodded and adjusted the glasses on his nose. The young soldier couldn't have been much past his late-20s, yet his hard and chiseled face and that faraway look in his eyes said he'd seen a lot more than his young years might have supposed. He ran a hand threw his blonde flattop haircut and shook his head, in exasperation more than anything.

"I was on one of the lower levels," Jake said, looking past Turn and probably past the previous few years as well. "My job wasn't critical, just working the switches for the trains that run down on Level 7. I didn't even know that something had happened up on Level 2 until the Reptilians began coming through about an hour later, doing the mop-up work."

"Jake, you don't have to—"

"No, it's alright," Jake said, waving away Ellis's words as well as the steadying hand that'd been moving toward his shoulder, "I *need* to do this."

Turn looked from Jake to Ellis and then back again, but remained quiet.

"They took out Lonnie and Chuck first, two of my best buds, guys that'd just been doing their shift and checking on one of the connection tubes as the routine called for. The problem was the Grays sent the lizards out to do their dirty work, and we all know they can't do anything right."

Jake laughed at that point as he looked at Ellis, and the Dutchman gave a slight smile. Jake's smile quickly faded and he continued.

"I heard the gunfire first, and it certainly wasn't M16 fire – that was clear right away. So I called it up to the next level, but there was no answer. That'd never happened before, and that's when I knew something was wrong."

"What'd you do?" Turn asked when Jake paused for several moments, lost in the memory of that day.

"I powered-up one of the spare trains and set it on auto-pilot for New York," Jake said with a sigh. "I ran, that's what I did."

"You got out, and gave us a helluva lot of information on what'd happened," Ellis said quickly, this time grabbing Jake by the shoulder and turning him to look in his eyes.

"Yeah, but—"

"Shut up!" Ellis shouted, slapping Jake across the face, hard. Jake's eyes went wide and he looked at the Dutchman in shock. "Listen, we're going to be heading back to Dulce tonight, and you're coming, Jake, and you're going to give those damn lizards some payback for Lonnie and Chuck, aren't you? Aren't you!"

"Damn right I am!" Jake said a moment later, fire in his eyes as he stared at his commander.

"Good," Ellis nodded. "Now let's get some chow, get some news, and then get equipped."

18 – A LOST SOUL

The final tray of dirty dishes was taken from the room and up ahead on the small stage of the cafeteria, Ellis stood up.

"Alright, alright…" he said, his arms up as he tried to quiet-down the more than two-dozen men that'd just eaten their dinner, perhaps the last for one or two of them, and maybe, Ellis pondered as he thought back on all the failed missions over the years, every single one of them.

"Quiet down!" Carl yelled from the bunched-together tables that the men were all seated around. It took another few moments, but quiet finally descended.

"As you men now know, we're moving tonight." Ellis paused and let the words sink in. The men had been training for weeks now, and some of them had even gone on a mission, but now it was the real thing. They all knew it could come at anytime, and now it had. "But we'll be doing so short one man, Captain Frank Burchak who died in Montana."

There were murmurings and a few prayers from the religious-types, but then the Dutchman pressed on.

"Frank was going to fly the X-22, the secret prototype we've been developing using alien technology, some of it given to us, some of it reverse engineered since '75. Frank had more hours on the thing than anyone besides those who designed it, Carl here being one."

Ellis nodded over his shoulder at Carl, who raised his hand slightly.

"Problem is, Carl can't fly that X-22 for shit," Ellis said, much to the chagrin of Carl but to the delight of those who saw the astronaut's face.

"Now, now…" Ellis said, a smile on his face and his hands up as if he expected Carl to run and barrel into him at any moment, "Carl's a great pilot and he'll make a helluva astronaut someday, but we need an *experienced* pilot at the controls of that craft."

"Oh," Carl said with a laugh, "and who the hell is that?"

DULCE BASE

"My son," Ellis said, "Mark Richards. He'll by flying the X-22."

"What?" several of the men said at once, none more so than Carl, now standing up at the front of the room next to him. Ellis turned to him.

"Everyone on this mission has their place, Carl – even you. We didn't count on losing Frank and–"

"But Ellis," Carl said, moving forward, his brow furrowed and his face looking confused, "Mark's dead."

"No," Ellis said, shaking his head.

"Shit," Tommy whispered beside Turn, and Turn looked around the crowded room to see several of the other men, mainly the commanders, echoing the same sentiment.

"Ellis, Mark died in 'Nam in '67…I saw his plane go down myself – I saw it explode!"

Ellis shook his head, the way you'd expect someone denying he'd just heard of the death of his son for the first time to shake *his* head. "No, Carl, you don't know what you saw."

Carl scoffed and looked down and shook his head. "Alright, Ellis, then if Mark's plane being blown out of the sky by a damn gook missile isn't what I saw, then you tell me what it was."

"It was a damn gook missile that you saw fly up and hit my Tiger, Carl," a voice said from the back of the room, causing all heads to turn toward a young man with black hair, a friendly face, and nearly the exact same features as the Dutchman standing before them, "it's just that you didn't see the Sirian TLV-series receptor vehicle come in and save my ass just in the nick of time."

Carl stood openmouthed, staring at an old friend, the son of his current friend, a man he was sure he'd seen die.

"You don't look a goddamn day older than you did that morning in May," Carl said, his eyes narrowing and his head moving back and forth slowly, as if he couldn't believe what he was seeing.

Mark shrugged. "I'm not, but that'll all change now that I'm back here on Earth."

"Uh…" Charlie said from the group of men staring on, "what the hell is going on here?"

Mark looked from Charlie to Ellis – his father, many in the room were just starting to realize – and cocked his head. "You want to tell 'em, dad, or should I?"

"Why not come up here and give the old man a hug first, huh?"

Mark walked forward, his smile increasing, and he and Ellis hugged tightly, the first time they'd done so in more than ten years.

"I never thought I'd see you again," Ellis whispered in Mark's ear.

"You always were wrong most of the time," Mark said, and they both laughed as they ended the embrace and looked back at the gathered men.

"Let's just say that I've been off-world, not necessarily of my own accord, but for my own betterment." He raised his hands up to quiet down the murmurs that produced, and continued on. "But now I'm back, and I know more about flying a UFO than any of you folks do, even you Stu, and you Eddie."

Both men nodded at that, not doubting Mark's words, for they both thought him dead as well, had attended the funeral for God's sake!

"And we're gonna need someone that knows how to fly one of those birds if we're to move in under a Bernarian ship and ride her tailwinds all the way into the hangar port undetected."

He paused and put his hands on his hips and began pacing back and forth, and if there was any doubt in the minds of the men that he was the Dutchman's son, it quickly vanished then.

"You men don't know me, but I'm asking you to trust me. I know that'll be hard, and that it's always hard having someone at your back you've never fought with before – hell, I know that firsthand myself! – but we don't have a whole lot of choices, now do we?"

"Carl could fly the X-22," Ellis said after a moment, a moment where no one said a word, "he helped design the damn thing, after all."

Mark smiled. "Oh, Carl...I've no doubt you could fly that thing better than anyone in this room – on any other night but tonight."

"And why do you say that?" Carl said, a smile on his face as he played along.

"Because you've never had two Ulterran fighters on your tail while racing into the needle of a canyon going 3,000 miles per hour and in slightly more gravity than we have here now. I have, and Bernarian ships are pretty damn similar to Ulterran ships, so I'm pretty confident I can ride *its* tail right into that hangar, allowing us to get in."

There was a long pause in the room after Mark's explanation, mainly because no one knew what he'd just said.

"It was gaining entry that always proved our downfall on the previous missions," Carl finally said from the front row of men.

"He's right," Ellis agreed, "and if we can gain entry to that port hangar we'll have access to those lower-level tube-tunnel controls."

Mark nodded. "And that means we can send in the other teams to hit the bottom while we're hitting the hell out of 'em on the top."

"A two front war," Turn said.

"At least two battles," Mark said, looking at him.

There was silence in the room as the men digested what they'd heard. No one objected, but then, no one really knew what to object *to*.

"That Bernarian ship's coming in just after the witching hour tonight," Mark said after another few moments had passed, looking at his father this time, "we better get moving."

19 – GETTING EQUIPPED

The men had filtered into one of the hangars on the edge of the base's airstrip, the one where the men's arsenal had been laid out. Table upon table was stretched out before them, all manner of machine guns, grenade launchers, side arms and even knives shining under the lights.

"Listen," Ellis said, stopping at the edge of one of the tables and waiting for the men to stop and turn back to him, "it's gonna be rough in there – I'm not gonna lie to you. Before we–"

"We've been briefed on the particulars of the operation, sir," Captain Sammy Williams said, giving him a straight look, not condescending at all, just plain and honest.

Ellis nodded. These men weren't interested in the particulars, they wanted to know what they needed to get the job done, done as quickly as possible, and with the most efficiency and least amount of error. In that regard it was all a numbers game, and the best score at the end would be the humans whatever and the aliens none. Ellis gave a sideways smirk, both at the thought of not suffering a casualty – they'd already lost one in Montana, hadn't they? – and the comment from Williams. But he nodded, and then flicked his chin forward, toward the table beside him.

"Those're the headsets we'll use," he said, coming up to the devices just as Carl reached down to pick one up, "they'll keep the team commanders in contact with their teams, and the commanders in contact with each other and the head command."

"But soldiers can't talk to soldiers, is that it?" Charlie asked, a bit of a laugh in his voice, although one that was taken rather quickly.

"Too much chatter," Ellis said, "it'd drown out everything and you wouldn't be able to concentrate."

"I'm fine with that," Donlon said, pushing past Charlie, "but what I want to know more about is the hardware."

Ellis nodded. It was no surprise the man leading the CAT-4 team would be interested in hardware – he was taking his men in on the tube trains and the fighting down in those lower-levels was bound to be intense.

"Same getup as last time," Ellis said, "M240 and AR-15 machine guns, Ingram MAC-10s for anyone that wants 'em, M203 China Lake grenade launchers, loose grenades and sidearms. We figure the more the better, your choice, you know what you like best."

"How 'bout my Uzis?" Aaron said. "I gotta have my Uzis."

"And I ain't goin' nowhere without my Colt's," Charlie said.

"No problem – they're yours," Ellis said.

"But what about their minds?" Walter asked, his tone more serious. He was leading CAT-2, the second team hitting the lower-levels from the trains. Many had seen what'd happened to Frank in Montana, and it'd only taken an hour of being back on base for the other men to spread the word to those who hadn't seen. No one wanted to experience *that* firsthand.

"You've got the six super soldiers," Ellis said, nodding toward the few in the room, "one on each team…at least."

"That ain't much use in a firefight when things get dicey and you gotta move quick," Fred said, a hard look in his eye and his face quivering with emotion, "a pair of guys can get separated *real* quick when that happens."

"And that's why you guys are the best, Fred," Ellis said, crossing his arms and taking on that no-nonsense look that said 'I've been down in the muck in German and Korea and 'Nam…what the hell do you want from me?'

Fred swallowed, his will to challenge the Dutchman shaken, but not gone entirely. It was his life on the line, after all.

"We might be the best, but there's never been a mission like this."

"And let's hope there'll never be another."

Ellis stared out at the men, giving each a hard look in the eye. He'd brook no dissent – it was all-in, or no-go…there was no pussy-footing around on this one."

"What I want to know," Tommy suddenly said, coming up from the far end of the room where he'd been perusing the weapons, that crazy and high voice of his setting nerves on edge, and getting right into Turn's face, "is what the hell I gotta do to blow one of them fuckin' Grays' heads apart like you did back there in 'ol Mon-tuck-*ee*!"

Turn gave a sideways look around at the others, then laughed. "Why, I just aimed at your ugly mug and fired, hopin' you'd be smart enough to duck."

The room exploded in laughter as Sammy, Ronnie, Johnny and Moses fell all over themselves and the younger white solders, most from the South, did the same nearby. Ellis even began laughing as well, until it looked like Robbie and Bobbie were about to topple the table holding the flash guns and he nearly rushed over before they got themselves under control.

"Shit," Tommy said with a chuckle, "I guess I'll have to try that then, huh?"

"You'll have that chance," Ellis said, a bit gruffly once again, "at 2200 tonight."

The men looked at one another quickly, their eyes saying it all – that was just two hours from now.

~~~

The men were walking down the hallway, heading to their respective team stations, ready to embark. Turn was taking up the rear – something he liked, since in combat he was always charging ahead – when Paul sidled up to him.

"Listen," Paul said, pulling Turn aside as they walked down the hallway, "don't buy into all of that back there."

Turn's eyes narrowed and he smiled and shook his head. "What are you talking about?"

"I'm talking about what they're telling the newbies, and what they're not telling us."

Turn narrowed his eyes further – he wasn't used to hearing Paul say so much. "What do you mean?"

Paul shook his own head and turned around, put his hands on his hips, and swore under his breath. Something was definitely bothering him.

"Shit, Turn – they're not gonna be ready, and if they're not, what's gonna happen to us, huh?"

"You're worried about the fear, is that it?" Turn said, moving forward and putting his hand on Paul's shoulder.

Turn and every other of the super soldiers knew full-well that the Grays had a…field of some sort around their body, one different from humans to the point where the merging of the two fields ended up creating physical symptoms, like the 'body terror' so many abductees and other contactees reported.

Paul nodded at Turn's words, and turned back to face him.

"The field around them is in direct opposition to ours," he said. "It's an anti-life field, one that comes directly from the Grays being on that devolutionary spiral. They're akin to soldiers of fortune, you know that, Turn, and 'offer' their advanced technology in trade for things they require." He shook his head. "Eisenhower should have been smarter than to get involved with them."

"But he wasn't."

Paul nodded. "But he wasn't."

"What do you want me to say?" Turn laughed. "I've heard it all before, seen it all before." He moved his arm around Paul's shoulder and started them both back down the hall. "How many missions have we been on, anyways? How many missions against these damn things from another world?"

"Oh, about five or six, I'd say, but–"

"Exactly – five or six. What are you worried about!"

"Turn, they're experts at manipulating both the human body and mind, and by using those fields to their advantage."

"And they require blood and other biological fluids to survive!" Turn said. "You heard Stan explaining it all this week, you know all about it...what's the big concern all of a sudden?"

Paul shook his head. "Maybe it's what happened back there to you in Montana, how you almost met those same helicopter blades. I just have a funny feeling about this one, Turn, just a funny feeling is all."

Turn looked at him and smiled. "Good, it wouldn't be right if you didn't."

20 – IN A FLASH

Outside the main Blue Lake hangar the X-22 was warming-up on the tarmac, the night as black as can be in that part of New Mexico. All twenty-nine of the men were assembled, including the three that would stay back and command the mission from afar, Ellis, Carl and General Anderholt. In just a few minutes the group would break apart in to their individual teams, and it'd be the last they'd see of one another until the planned-forty-minute mission was complete…if they were lucky. Ellis looked around at the men and tried not to play out in his mind which would be skilled enough to come back and which wouldn't, but he couldn't help it – three wars had taught him the importance of weighing the future, even if a good-deal of luck always seemed to throw the calculations off.

"Listen up," Ellis said loudly and in a no-nonsense voice, "I'm only going to say this once, so listen good."

The joking and carousing continued for a few more moments, then generally died down. The Dutchman began.

"Everything was going according to plan with these bases until May 1, 1975. On that day all hell broke loose."

Tommy cracked a laugh, expecting a good story.

"The plan was rubbish, right from the get go, the treaties nothing – the aliens never kept their end of the bargain. That technology we were promised? Nope, only allowed in the bases and then under intense supervision. And those men and women that we'd allowed the aliens to take and then return, the original abductees? Some you heard about the Betty and Barney Hill case and you might have seen the old black and white videos of the two. But they were the exception – more and more were never seen or heard from again. Later we learned out what'd become of them, and it wasn't a pretty picture, not in the least."

Ellis took in a deep breath and you could have heard a pin drop, the room was so quiet.

"It was when they began to manipulate our thoughts," he continued with a shake of his head, "that we really knew we'd gotten the short end of the stick. The aliens had never wanted to give us anything in the first place, it'd all been smoke and mirrors, a way for them to gain access to our minds and then our bodies and then eventually our society. High-level members of our government and military were brainwashed, had chips implanted in their brains, and sometimes were even cloned and replaced outright. The worst was when they had their very souls taken, God knows where. And the army of clones and half-human hybrids, things that would make the task of taking over the world a lot easier for the aliens?" Ellis sighed. "We knew we had to fight back, but in the end it wasn't us that fired the first shot.

"It happened in the tunnels below us, when two Ret Four Grays demanded that an entire group of armed military personnel unload their weapons and then drop them. When the commander asked why the entire squad was killed, each with a shot to the head, although the aliens had no guns and from what we could tell from the cameras and the bodies we recovered later, these were nothing more than psychic shots, some kind of mind blast that killed.

The idea was that the Grays used their minds to do it, somehow through the bio-chemical circuit board that's up in those big heads with huge black eyes. They figured out how to channel electromagnetic energy via specific neural patterns and pathways. It makes them virtually unstoppable.

"So how the hell do we kill 'em?" Charlie asked.

Carl nodded at the six men that'd stepped forward. "That's what we got the super soldiers for."

"It was made clear to us after that initial massacre," Ellis continued, "that the Grays were not our allies as they'd originally claimed, but conquerors come in disguise. Just because one officer questioned the need for our human forces to disarm themselves, the faux treaty was realized. It was clear that they Grays had to maintain discipline at all costs, even if that meant we knew they had no regard for us at all."

There were murmurings of discontent, for it truly was a depressing tale.

"Not everyone was killed, though," Ellis continued, to the raised eyebrows of some of the men. He glanced over at someone that others couldn't see, then nodded before continuing. "I'm going to say some things we haven't told the groups before, because this time it's different. Those guns the humans had been told to disarm weren't regular guns, they were the flash guns that were just then coming into use by our forces, something that'd been a gift from the Nordics, another alien race, more enlightened and advanced than the Grays, and one that actually has our interests at heart. It wasn't forty-four that were killed that day, but sixty-eight. Of those that died, twenty-two were completely vaporized as the flash guns of the Grays were turned upon us. But more than just a single survivor managed to get away. In all, nineteen escaped back into the tunnels, and since the attack occurred on Level 2, it meant they had a good change of getting out, and twelve managed to do so. To this day they're in hiding, crashing in motels and surfing couches, but alive, and safe…and ready to fight in any way they can."

Tommy laughed. "Well, then where the hell are they?"

"Their time will come," Walter said, and from the tone of his voice, it was almost as if he'd been one of the men himself.

"Just one Gray was killed in that massacre, a lucky shot from one of our soldiers," Ellis said, picking up the story and bringing it to its end. "The thing wasn't vaporized, but it died a slow and agonizing death, you can be assured of that."

"How many of you men have seen a flash gun?" Stu asked, stepping forward from the front of the group, his voice echoing off the far hangar wall. The men grew silent in just a moment, so tense and on edge and just ready to go were they.

"How many of you have seen this?" Stu asked, holding up a small metal rod.

"Colonel…I've already got a pen," Major Jake Zates said in that dead-humored voice of his.

"They're flash guns," Stu said above the few chuckles as he picked one up and weighed it in his hand, "although they were originally called the Armorlux weapon. It's an advanced beam weapon that can operate on three different phases: stun, levitate and paralyze."

Stu held it up for the others to see. It resembled a flashlight, with a black glass conical inverted lens. On the side were three recessed knobs in three curved grooves and each knob was a different size.

"Although we all know that 'paralyze' is just short for 'kill,' don't we, Stu?"

Stu looked at Lieutenant Colonel Eddie Okamata. "That's not quite accurate. On the higher position on the same mode it can create a temporary kind of death, one that I assure you any doctor would certify as clinically dead. What he wouldn't know, however, is that the person's – or *thing's* in some cases – that the person's life essence is actually lingering in some strange limbo, some kind of terrible state of non-death. In one to five hours the person will begin to wake up, or revive if you will, slowly at first, as the bodily functions start up once again, and then a few minutes onward, consciousness returns, followed by full awareness."

"God, sounds awful!"

Stu smiled as he looked at Lewie. "What the Grays use it for might be worse. It's in *that* mode that the alien scientists use to re-program the human brain and plant false information. When the person awakens, they 'recall' this false and implanted information as knowledge they've gained through real-life experiences. There *is* no way for a person to learn the truth after that, they're simply too far gone. They'll never believe you, will always resist. They're lost to us."

There were murmurings to that, and Stu gave an inward smile, knowing he'd made each and everyone of the men aware of the dangers of this weapon, and the need to obliterate anything holding one.

"Tell them about the highest position," Mark pressed.

Stu frowned, but shrugged and pointed at the smallest button on the flash gun, and also the one closest to the top.

"This *is* the kill button, or more aptly, the vaporize button. It'll leave nothing more than a small, barely discernable pile of black dust and ash where the person or thing was just standing."

No one said anything to that, just gulped a bit and hoped they'd never be on the receiving end.

PART III
21 – THE X-22

Blue Lake
Thursday, May 24, 1979

The X-22 was quite the bird, if you wanted to call it that. The first thing anyone noticed were the huge tilting ducted fans, two on the forward 22-foot wings and two on the rear 39-foot wings. Together the four three-bladed propellers gave the plane vertical and/or short take-off and landing capability, or V/STOL as it was called. The X-22 achieved that by synchronizing a wave-interconnection system with four gas turbines that were also located on the rear wings. When the turbines fired the plane could lift off, and steering was achieved by tilting the propeller blades in conjunction with the elevators and ailerons of the thrust system. Each of the turbines could produce 1,267 hp, allowing the X-22 to travel at 254 mph, or just over 400 km/h...a lot less than the 326 mph she was supposed to get by design.

Not that that mattered to any of the men standing there in awe of the craft, which looked like something most had never seen.

"The X-22 program was cancelled in 1966," a voice said from behind them, and the men turned to see Captain Mark Richards approaching, "although that was just the *official* version, of course."

"So that's what we'll by flying into the port in, huh?" Turn asked.

"Aye, and flying out in too...if you're lucky."

Mark gave the flight engineer and mission commander a hard stare, then nodded. "We can manage."

22 – BEFORE THE ATTACK

Ellis looked on as the men got into the X-22, his son leading the way. At least with Charlie, Walter and Donlon leading the three land-force CATs the men knew what to expect, the Dutchman thought to himself. Each of the men had been tested in battle and they knew their teammates well – they'd often been beside them there in the thick of it, and some had even fought as a team in Montana. The third CAT team, however, the one that his son would be leading and which the entire success of the mission depended upon, would be blazing the trail for the larger Fast Action Team and Clean Up Team coming in on their tail, would be attacking under the command of a man most had never fought beside, but whom most *had* heard about.

Mark Richards was nearly as much a legend as his old man, and some said more so. The Dutchman's son was well-known in black ops circle and two things were beyond question: the younger Richards had proven himself in combat, and he'd never asked his men to do anything he wasn't ready to do. More importantly, he'd never left a man behind.

While his missions had almost always been so top secret that nobody knew details, the rumors and trail of evidence was more than clear to any in the know. What's more, it was rumored that he'd been off-world, perhaps even to a distant alien planet. When it came to the Richards', anything was possible.

The only problem for the command chain was Richards' reputation for being something of a loose cannon when it came to following orders that he didn't think were in the best interest of his men or the mission - a fact that just made him more popular with his men.

Few of those things were going through the younger Richards' mind as he climbed into the X-22 cockpit and settled behind the controls. Turn was beside him and Andy and Billy just over his shoulder. It seem the appropriate time for a prayer.

"I am a Commando," he began, "as my brother Commandos before me, I am proud to step into history as a member of the Air Force Special Operations Command."

"I will walk with pride with my head held high, my heart and attitude will show my allegiance to God, country and comrades," the other men joined in from behind. "When unable to walk another step, I will walk another mile. With freedom my goal, I will step into destiny with pride and the Air Force Special Operations Command."

Mark glanced over at Turn out of the corner of his eye and smiled, then powered up the X-22, gave the order for the helicopter to follow, then pushed the strange tilt-rotor aircraft to its flight limits in a wild high speed bank over the runway that impressed the hell out of the troops still on the ground...not to mention set the tone for the mission.

"Woo-hoo!" Billy shouted from the back seats as they shot into the air, already going 180 mph according to the instruments just past Mark's fingertips.

Over the earphones and speakers came first his voice, then the voice of the team members with him in the X-22, singing the Air Force hymn. In the Puma helicopter on the ground, Moses and the rest of the men of the CUT team started into the song as well.

"Up and away, into the wild blue yonder!" the men shouted as they saw the X-22 shoot forth into the dark night, toward the Archuleta Mesa and the secret underground Dulce base.

"We can't very well let that bunch smash open the Gates of Hell without the rest of us being right behind them," shouted Moses as he lifted the helicopter off the ground, the X-22 nearly out of sight already.

"Damn right we can't," Aaron said beside him. "Fire this bird up – we've got some aliens to kill."

23 – DOWN IN THE TUNNELS

Down in the lower levels of Blue Lake base Combat Assault Teams (CAT) 1, 2 and 4 stood outside the double-side platform where the tube train was set to arrive.

"Looks like a damn subway station in New York!" Second Lieutenant David Tish grumbled, something the other men had come to expect was all that was possible from him (they'd yet to see him in combat, after all).

"It'll take you to New York," Donlon said as he checked his M16 assault rifle for the tenth or so time.

"So don't tell me–"

Jake's words were cutoff as 'wooshing' sound could suddenly be heard in the distance, coming from behind them. Everyone turned to see the light of a train coming, and then a moment later they turned around to see one coming on the opposite side of the platform.

"Tube 1 is you guys, Walter," Donlon said to Captain Walter Leathers with a nod, then raised his arm toward Tube 2 across the way and looked to his own men, "and we'll go this way."

Everyone nodded and gathered their things and started to board the trains.

"There's no one driving!" Bobbie said with a laugh of surprise when the train finally stopped and he was able to see into the main engineer's compartment.

"They've been fully-automated since they were installed," Walter said, ushering him onto the train, which was really nothing more than two cars pulled by the main engine, if you even wanted to call it that.

"Thing looks more like a bumper car to me," David grumbled as he got onto Tube Train 2.

"Won't feel that way when it starts moving," Robbie said, "not if they go Mach 2 like Colonel Donlon said in the briefing."

David just frowned to that, but got onto the train and settled down. Across the way the men of Walter's team did the same.

"Good luck, Walter!" Donlon called out over the platform.

"You too, Roger!" Walter called back, and then there was an audible beeping for a moment, the doors slammed shut, and the two trains started down the tracks.

24 – TAKING OFF

Desert – East of the Jicarilla Apache Nation Reservation, New Mexico
Thursday, May 24, 1979

The X-22 raced over the desert at over 250 mph, the bottom of its rotor tubes missing the rocks by less than twenty feet at times. Turn stared out the window as New Mexico flew by at an unbelievable rate. First they'd passed by the Rio Grand Del Norte National Park and then the Carson National Forest. They skirted along Highway 111, but stayed high enough and far enough away that they weren't noticed, not that anyone could see the black craft with no lights anyways. After that they'd turned north a bit, the better to skirt around the Jicarilla Apache Indian Reservation. It was then that they'd dropped altitude, coming in down to almost touch the desert floor. It was that fast-moving terrain that Turn looked at, seated now in the back with the others, but he also listened as Captain Mark Richards, the Dutchman's son, regaled them with his tales.

"...and that's the fastest I've flown," he said, just finishing up a story of a race between two planets that none of the men had ever heard of, but which didn't prevent both Andy and Billy in the back from staring, mouths agape.

Turn frowned, shook his head at the two seated opposite him in the small back-seating area of the X-22, then turned back to look up at the Dutchman's son sitting in the pilot's seat...or at least that's how he thought of Captain Richards, a man he didn't really know, none of them knew. Biting his lip and firming his resolve, he cleared his throat.

"Sir," he began, and Mark stopped fiddling with a few controls and turned his head about to look at him.

"Yes...question...?"

"Turn" he began, saying his name which he expected the seemingly-cocky and cock-sure young man to have forgotten already. "Well, sir, it's just that what you said about the dates and the ships and...it just didn't make sense."

"*What* didn't make sense?" Mark asked, his eyes narrowing slightly and his mouth tightening. Turn thought about shaking his head and laughing the whole thing off, but something told him Mark wouldn't let him.

"You mentioned something about 'their ships,' and I just thought that from your tone you were implying something, oh, I don't know...larger, than what we'd be thinking of when we think of UFO."

Mark nodded and then smiled. "The first Gray motherships came over a three year period, from 1787 to 1789...right as the French Revolution was getting underway. They'd sent probe ships earlier – 1645 was the first recorded sighting from Europe – and this lasted until 1767. At the time it was just thought of as a mistake in the evolving science of telescopy, this moon appearing and then disappearing again – no one thought much of it."

"But..." Turn said, sensing it was appropriate.

"But," Mark nodded, "it wasn't a moon, and those three moons that appeared in the late 1780s weren't moons either. They kept coming, too – another mothership near Mercury in 1789, the Sun in 1859, and Mars in 1894. Besides that the moon of Pluto called Kerberos, or Vulcan now, is actually a mothership and has been there since the 1850s, although we haven't officially 'discovered' it yet, that won't happen until...."

"Until what, sir..."

"Never mind," Mark said quickly and with a laugh, "now where was I? Oh yes...in 1878 an Andromedan an a Pleiadian mothership came in, ostensibly to monitor the Grays who'd been taking quite a bit of interest in our Sun at that time." Mark trailed-off and stared-off into the distance before continuing, as if talking to himself. "It could also be that they were interested in the Reptilians, who first appeared in 1783 on the moon. They liked it enough that they came back in 1787 and set up their base their. Intrepid photographers were able to get shots of their ships in 1892, 1894, and 1912. After that they took greater pains to cloak themselves, seeing as our technology was 'advancing,' so to say."

Mark look back over his shoulder at Turn, then broke out into a smile and laugh. "Here I am, talking to myself again...you really must excuse me."

"It's perfectly all right, it's just...I think I have more questions than before I asked."

"The good ones always do – now about what's coming up," he said with a smile, then turned back around even further this time, making sure both Andy and Billy were paying attention. They were. "What we've got coming up, boys, is some serious security measures, having to do with that sonic weaponry system the Grays have."

"We were briefed on that," Andy said.

"Good, then you know we have to disable it before the other teams can do anything, don't you?"

Turn looked across at the two younger soldiers, and all three nodded.

"Good, because—"

WOOSH!

There was an amazing woosh of air and the X-22 shook about, so much so that Turn thought they'd been struck by something and were going down. A moment later a shimmering blackness appeared before them, blacker even than the surrounding night and desert floor.

"There she is," Mark said to himself but loud enough for the others to hear, his teeth gritted but his mouth smiling, "right on schedule."

25 – DRAWING NEAR

"Five miles," Aaron said, turning a few knobs and then looking over at Captain Moses Cochrane.

"Check," the pilot of the Puma helicopter said, then swiveled his head a bit to shout back to the men in the rear, "maintaining our 5-mile distance from CAT-3 and about 100 miles out."

"Hear that, boys?" Ronnie said with a laugh. "Just 100 more miles and we'll be blastin' aliens!"

Sergeant Jerry Carol and Corporal Jonny Wake didn't look too thrilled at that prospect, but beside them Sergeant Paul Carson was all smiles.

"Yeah, real easy for you to be happy," Sergeant Lewie Yates said from across the floor of the helicopter, "you're one of the super soldiers – you got nothin' to worry about."

"You don't either, not if you stay close to me," Paul said.

"Everyone needs to stay close," Eddie said, "at least until we get those HUB doors blown and those sonic weapons systems taken out."

"And then what?" Johnny asked.

"Then we open up on 'em with everything we got," Stan said with a smile, though it was hard to see from under that bushy handlebar mustache of his.

"Well, *you* men will," Stu said, his usual white professor's jacket switched out for a set of Delta Force black, "Eddie, Ronnie and Stan will be trying to—"

"Contact!" Aaron shouted from the cockpit, his fist held up. "The X-22 just made contact!"

~~~

Captain Mark Richards gritted his teeth and pulled back on the controls of the X-22, thankful the three men in the back couldn't see how close he'd just come to crashing into the UFO after it'd suddenly descended upon them. Now he was hovering just over it, closer than he had been to the desert floor, about ten feet. And up ahead was Dulce Base.

It'd been just another patch of blackness on an already black horizon, but then there was a shimmer and an open pair of blast doors were suddenly there before them, still about a mile off, but coming up fast, the yellow light spilling out into the darkness of the night as the holographic blanketing projectors were turned off and the base was revealed to the world, however fleeting it might be.

"What is that?" Billy said from the back.

"That's Dulce," Mark said, his knuckles white on the controls. They were half a mile out and he was still too high. If he was going to then he'd have to do it…

Mark swiveled the controls and brought them down right on top of the alien craft they were riding in with, the one that was meant to block them from view. It was working, so far, and now just inches from the top of the craft and the doors coming up and–"

"Now!" Mark shouted, and turned the X-22 to the right just as they were about to enter the Dulce Base port.

It was a sight, a huge floor with a command building of some sort dead center, row upon row of small, triangular…fighter craft was all Turn could think of them as…lined up all across the port's floor. The walls looked made of concrete and metal and stretched more than a hundred feet up to the ceiling above them. But what really had Marks' attention, Turn could tell, were the pair of mounted-laser guns on the wall ahead of them.

Mark swerved to the right, putting the alien UFO between them and that gun while putting the second right in front of them. He pushed a button, unleashing two Hellfire missiles right toward that mounted laser as it began to swivel toward them. It'd made it a few inches before the Hellfires blew it to pieces.

"Woo-hoo!" Mark shouted, and Turn almost expected him to reach up for a cowboy hat that wasn't there, waving it about in glee. Instead he cut the speed of the X-22 dramatically by tilting the thrusters and bringing them down. In the same motion he re-aimed the missile guidance system, hit the button unleashing two more Hellfire missiles, and took care of the other mounted laser just like that.

"Goddamn!" Andy said from the back of the X-22, and beside him Billy nodded, wide-eyed.

"Not so fast," Mark said from the cockpit, and turned them about quickly. The men in the back couldn't see it, but the alien UFO that they'd rode in on was trying to turn about in an attempt to get out of the now-compromised entry-port to Dulce.

SHOOM! SHOOM!

"Shit," Mark said as two lasers fired what looked to Turn to be just inches above the X-22's glass cockpit canopy. They didn't seem to faze Mark too much, however, for he just re-angled the X-22 and fired off another Hellfire, then gave it a little pitch and yaw and fired off another.

Turn didn't know a thing about flying hovercrafts, but he was pretty certain he knew what another two mounted lasers being blown to hell sounded like.

~~~

"Goddamn, there ain't gonna be nothing left!" Aaron said from the helicopter that was now just a mile from the still-open Dulce Base blast doors.

"Better find some wood to knock on," Moses said beside him, "because I have a feeling there'll be plenty."

He angled the Puma downward and just a dozen feet from the desert floor and they covered the remaining distance to the Dulce port quickly.

"Bring 'er down easy," Aaron said beside him as they flew into the port.

It was a rectangular port, really nothing more than a large underground parking lot, this one just for UFOs. There were several lined up in 'parking spots,' lighted-off areas that almost seemed to conform to the shape of the ship sitting in them, and the area could obviously afford much larger craft, for the ceiling was more than a hundred feet off the floor.

"There!" Aaron said, pointing out the window to a clear spot on the floor, just before and below where the X-22 and the alien transport craft were still hovering, and turning about it looked like.

"Got it," Moses said, then brought the bird down.

"All right," Aaron shouted, ripping off his headset and jumping back to the other men, "let's hit 'em hard!"

26 – MAKING ENTRY

Dulce Port (Level 1) – Dulce Secret Base, New Mexico
Thursday, May 24, 1979

The attack was textbook, with the CAT-3 forces blowing an entry into the port and taking full control of their landing zone within 55 seconds of the X-22 breaching the port. Hovering, the X-22 continued to use its rockets and guns to rake any enemy weapons in the port area, silencing them before the Air Force helicopter piloted by Moses Cochrane started to enter the open port doors.

Moses brought the bird in fast and put her down on the main floor of the chamber where the troops would have the cover of a nearby disk as they ran for the passenger entry hatch. Mark knew it was time.

"All right, you bastard!" he said, his teeth gritted but his smile wide. "See how you handle this!"

Turn's eyes were wide as he watched the alien disc-shaped craft begin to move forward, most likely trying to dart out of there. Instead Captain Richards brought the X-22 forward and then jerked left on the controls, something that caused the left wing of the X-22 to slam downward toward the alien ship. At the last second he kicked the props into a full downdraft, nearly flipping the UFO over onto its top.

"Ha!" he laughed, but all the while he was struggling with the controls. "Hang on boys!" he shouted back to them next.

"Shit!" Turn said, then grabbed onto the hand-straps and braced himself.

Mark managed to straighten-out the X-22 but he was coming down, and would have to land the vehicle. It's tires hit the port's pavement hard and they bounced a bit, but once again they were lined-up perfectly with the alien craft, enough so that Mark could unleash two Hellfires toward it. The craft managed to dodge one but the second hit it straight on and it fell a good forty feet, and right on top of a few triangle-shaped craft that had been sitting there.

"Woo!" Mark shouted again. "Took out two fighters with that one – woo-ee!"

~~~

"And...she's down!"

Command Sergeant Major Aaron Haney looked from Moses in the cockpit to Jerry by the helicopter's large bay door, and nodded.

The door was already thrown open by the time he yelled 'open 'er up' and Sergeant Paul Carson jumped out, his M240 leading the way.

BOOM!

Paul looked over as the alien UFO Captain Richards had tailed-in on crashed down atop some other type of alien craft. He quickly directed his attention back toward the HUB doors, which were the main entryway into the base from the port. If those were closed to them then the base was effectively sealed off. What's more, they still had to secure the small port facility command post, the one that housed the may well house the sonic controls for the entire base – he wasn't convinced they were only on the lower level. It was a lot of shit to handle, and Paul let off his frustration by bringing the machine gun up and firing at a Gray coming out from behind the side of the command post, the first he'd seen yet. The thing had obviously been expecting something to happen that didn't, for its body seemed to slink down and it was just trying to back off when Paul opened-up on it.

"Damn!" Johnny said as he jumped down beside Paul, his sawed-off Remington shotgun up and aiming in the direction the Gray had been. "You split that one's head clean in half!"

"Happens," Paul said matter-of-factly, and a moment later Jerry and Lewie were down on the concrete of the port as well.

"Let's secure this facility!" Aaron shouted from inside the helicopter, his two Uzis held at his sides, just aching to be used.

"What about the others?" Paul called out as Aaron jumped down.

"They'll wait 'till we secure the area then work their magic."

Paul smiled. "Then it's time for me to work mine."

He started toward the port command post fifty yards away, the other five men fast on his heels, guns a' blazin'.

27 – THE BATTLE FOR COMMAND

"Go, go, go!" Jerry shouted, his arm waving as Johnny, Lewie and then Aaron all rushed past. He put his AR-15 assault rifle to his eye, or close enough as his large, black-framed glasses would allow, and fired.

Coming just around the bend and raising up what looked like a pen was a Gray. Jerry's shot took it in the shoulder, but since its frame was so small and the force of the gun so much, the blast took of the thing's whole side. Blowing out his breath in relief that the alien hadn't gotten the flash gun up in time, Jerry started forward.

"There it is," Paul was saying when Jerry got up against a parked alien UFO of some sort, another one beside it so they had some cover.

"See it," Aaron said, emptying out the clips from his guns and then re-inserting them again, a nervous habit he had.

"How are you gonna—"

Lewie's words were cut off as a laser or weapon of some sort blasted right into the UFO near their heads.

"Sombitch!" Jonny said, those large black lips of his quivering in anger. He grabbed hold tightly of his shotgun, jumped up, and fired a shot off in the direction the laser blast had come, then another and another before falling back down.

"They're movin' in," he said, his eyes darting this way and that.

"It's alright," Paul said, his voice level and calm, like always, "we just have to get to that door, get it open, and that's that – the controls to the sonic and all the rest of Dulce are in there."

"The sonic – that's down below on Level 7!" Jerry shouted.

Paul shook his head. "It's in here, too – I know it."

"Then let's move," Jerry said, narrowing his eyes at him, and started to rise up, "you men move and I'll cover the rear – get that door open!"

The others didn't have much choice in the matter – Jerry jumped up and began firing his machine gun rapidly, those thick glasses of his obscuring his eyes, but not the wicked grin on his face.

"Move!" Aaron shouted, and the others took off, Lewie charging forth across the open floor toward the command center thirty yards away, Paul and Johnny and then Aaron behind him.

"C'mon," Aaron shouted once they'd moved a bit and Jerry was still behind, shooting at the Grays behind them, "we can't get too far from Paul!"

Aaron kept back-stepping as he said it, and within another moment he was already ten yards from Jerry.

"Jerry, c'mon!" he shouted again, but it was too late. Paul was far enough away now, as well as the protection his mental blocking ability afforded. One of the Grays somewhere in the distance or firing upon them from afar, sensed this, and began to work its mental muscle.

"Paul!" Aaron shouted, and ahead of him Johnny and then Paul turned about.

"Damn!" Paul said under his breath, the first that any of them had heard him swear. Ahead of him Jerry was struggling, his AR-15 beginning to move back to point at his head, his arms fighting a losing battle to prevent his body from unintentionally killing itself.

"Fuck this!" Johnny said, and grabbed one of the grenades fastened at his belt. He lobbed it up and over where Jerry had been shooting, and a few moments later it exploded.

BOOM!

Not waiting to see if that did the trick or not, Johnny rushed forth and started firing into the smoky area past the parked UFOs where the alien fire had been coming from.

"Got him!" Lewie shouted, and Johnny looked over his shoulder to see Jerry down on the ground, and once again under command of his own faculties. Paul was near.

"Let's get to that door before this happens again!" he shouted at them, although it sounded more like the way an average person talked.

It was clear that what Grays there were in the port area of the base hadn't been expecting an attack, and were now scurrying to play catch up. What's more, already several of their number had been gunned-down, the initial Gray by Paul and then the one by Jerry, not counting however many Johnny managed to blow to hell or whatever version of it the things had. It was for that reason that the five special forces soldiers managed to race across the thirty yards of open port hangar floor to reach the small command facility building set square in the center of the large space. No further shots came, and within seconds Johnny was fiddling with the controls.

"C'mon!" Lewie shouted, looking around nervously, his two Colt .45s held up and at the ready.

"Blow it!" Jerry shouted a second later.

"We need this building secure," Paul said calmly, giving the two men an even look.

"Got it!" Johnny said a moment later, and there was an audible click, hiss of air, and then the door opened. The men rushed inside.

~~~

"They're in!" Eddie shouted, clapping his hands together. He and the other main scientists, engineers and astronauts of the FAT Team were still in the helicopter, which was still just sitting out in the open.

"They'll have it secure in a minute, two at the most," Stan said, his eyes sparkling with a mischievous from under that large mustache.

Ronnie smiled at him. "Then let's get to work."

The men bolted from the helicopter and out toward the three lines of parked UFO fighter craft on the other side of the hangar.

"No...hey...shit!" Stu said from his spot in the helicopter, then held up his hand to stop Eddie from trying to rush after them. "No, let them go – they know what they're doing...I hope."

~~~

"What the hell is all this?" Lewie said once they were inside the command center.

"Never seen a computer before?" Paul smiled at him, what Lewie figured was the closest he'd ever come to a laugh.

"No, er...yes, er...you know!"

"These are complex systems, devised to keep unwanteds out and the better-not-seens in," Aaron said as he huddled up to one control console and began looking at numbers and dials and knobs and readouts.

"What's what?" Jerry said with a laugh. "All this junk looks the same to me."

"They're servers," Paul said, not taking his eyes from scanning the various controls in a very quick and thorough way, "they hold all the information you could ever want *and* keep the base safe. And if any one of these things ever–"

Johnny narrowed his eyes and looked over at Paul, who'd stopped mid-sentence for some reason.

"Here it is!" the super soldier said in excitement. "The sonic controls!"

"Well I'll be damned," Aaron shouted. "Switch it off!"

"Alright," Paul said right back, and a moment later flipped off the seven yellow-lit switches all in a row. There was an audible hum, a lowering of frequency, a depressing drone.

"Sounds like you just killed something," Lewie laughed.

"Yeah," Aaron said with a smile, pointing out the one small window on the side of the wall near the door. There they could see the flickering of the hologram concealing the very blast doors they'd come in through. What's more, they now saw that those blast doors were in fact holograms themselves. They knew this when they just winked right out of existence.

Jerry laughed and the others looked to him, looked to see that wicked grin of his.

"Time to rock and roll," he smiled.

28 – DISARRAY DOWN BELOW

Dulce Platform (Level 7)
Thursday, May 24, 1979

"What's that?" Major John Bingham said, his eyes darting up above to where the lights were on the train's ceiling, lights that were just then beginning to flicker, winking in and out. As usual, he had his lucky Vietnam combat helmet on, the dull and faded green a stark contrast to the black special forces and Delta Force uniforms all of the men were wearing. He said it brought him luck, however, and none of the men were going to begrudge him that.

Sammy and Tommy looked at one another, then smiled.

"It's the sonic," Sammy said, looking to John. "They just secured the port above us – the security systems have all been switched off!"

"Shit," Tommy spat, "I thought we were doin' that!"

Chargin' Charlie, the leader of CAT-1–the first team that'd reach the lower levels of Dulce – leaned back and smiled. That was what they were waiting for, the shutting off of power so they could move about freely, not having to worry about a hidden force of energy slicing them in half or trapping their mind or any of the other atrocities that Dulce possessed. What the hell did it matter who shut it off?

"One minute!" Sammy shouted out, glancing down at his pocket watch again.

In just one minute they'd be pulling into the main tube platform of Dulce, located on Level 7 and connecting to other tubes leading to other underground bases all over the world. The area was key, both for their quick infiltration and destroy mission, and their long-term goals of taking the area back.

Suddenly there were tunnel lights out the train's windows, and then flickering as they entered an open area. The men huddled closer to the set of double doors facing toward that area, an area that opened up to reveal a double-platform with a long strip running in between two sets of tracks.

"We're here," Tommy said.

Charlie peered out the window, then let his eyes go wide. There before them were dozens of Grays, all standing about in the small platform, some working or even 'talking' by the look of it. None of them seemed to notice that a small group of armed humans was rushing right into their midst.

The train stopped, there was a beep just like any subway train in New York, and the doors slid open.

If there was ever a calm before the storm, Charlie thought, this was surely it. The four men of CAT-1 stood there, huddled in the small doorway of the train, their guns held up in front of their chests, their eyes wide, and their resolve waning. It seemed like an eternity but was actually less than a few seconds, seconds in which the clusters of Grays standing about on the platform slowly turned their attention, then heads, then bodies their way. There was no discernible reaction, no altering of facial features – which Ellis and Carl had pretty much made plain was quite impossible anyways – an no real indication that anything was remiss. That is, until one of the Grays in a tight pocket of three just a few yards to their right suddenly whipped around to look at his two companions. Charlie didn't need to see facial features change to know the thing was surprised, and that they were found out.

"They know they can't hurt us!" Charlie yelled to the men beside him.

"Not with us two standing here," Tommy smiled, bringing his M16 up to his face to better take aim, "now let's give 'em a little taste of the American way!"

The men didn't need to be told twice, and a split-second later the platform was echoing with gunfire.

Tommy got the first shot off, right at the Gray that'd turned about in surprise to 'talk' with its two companions. The burst of three M16 assault rifle bullets hit right in the plum center of that big 'ol head of the Gray, and that greenish-blood of theirs flew all over its two companions as the creature fell to the floor, dead before it even hit.

It may have been surprise in the eyes of the creatures' two companions, but it might just as well have been fear. Neither John nor Sammy was really sure nor really cared, they just pulled their triggers and sent the two things down to the platform, one with several AR15 bullets in its head, the other with its head blown clean off, Sammy's Mossberg Model 590 shotgun blast still echoing around the cavernous area they were in.

That did it – seeing three of their number go down in just a few seconds, all of their psychic attacks failing, and human commandos coming in for the kill – and the Grays broke and ran.

"It's a turkey shoot!" John shouted out with a laugh, then brought his AR15 to his eye once again, tilted his dull, green helmet back, aimed and then fired. Another Gray went down, a bullet in the side of its big head, the easiest target John had ever fired at, and he'd been firing a lot since growing up down in the bayous of south Georgia.

"You ain't seen nothin' yet!" Tommy said with a laugh, then angled his M203 upwards and fired. The grenade launched forth, made an arc in the air, and then came down right in the midst of a group of Grays that'd been trying to run right past them from the other end of the platform. The four beings were thrown into the air, shrapnel from the grenade and the platform digging into their frail frames and tearing them apart.

"Whooee! Tommy shouted in glee at the sight of his handiwork, though the sound was immediately drowned-out by the sound of another approaching tube train.

"Here they are!" Charlie shouted as he brought up his machine gun and fired off another burst, taking down yet another Gray that'd been rushing right in front of them in its frantic need to get off the platform.

Sure enough, the second tube train was pulling up to the platform, the one that'd set-out from Blue Lake just a couple minutes behind the four men of CAT-1.

"It's party time!" Sammy said as he fired off another shot from his Mossberg, taking out a Gray and a good portion of a second that'd been running beside it. He lowered the shotgun and nodded across the platform at the doors beginning to open on the tube train opposite them.

"Fucking-A!" Corporal Bobbie Baker shouted, the first of CAT-2 out of the tube train as the doors opened, his Heckler & Koch HK1 light support machine gun opening up upon a group of straggling Grays that'd been all the way at the other end of the platform and rushing furiously toward the exit there. The German machine gun's bullets ripped into them and tore flesh and bone and left a helluva mess all over that end of the platform. Bobbie just laughed and took aim at another group.

Within seconds Captain Walter Leathers, Lieutenant Colonel Emil Wiseman, and Major Jake Zates were beside him, each firing away at a pocket of Grays here, a lone individual running there, or even one of the poor bastards that'd merely been wounded. Each man knew of the psychic capabilities of these creatures, either seeing it firsthand in Montana or hearing about it afterward, and each wasn't going to leave anything alive that could try something funny when their team's back was turned.

Colt AR-15s sang with German Heckler & Koch's and the occasional grenade or shotgun blast for accompaniment. The men played their symphony of destruction, hitting all the right notes and leaving the Grays that'd been on the platform hopelessly outgunned. For with the super soldier on each of the Combat Assault Teams, there was just no way the

Grays could do anything with their minds – their most powerful weapon – not one damn thing.

"Boom!" Charlie yelled as he dropped the last Gray in front of him, a spindly bastard that'd been trying to rush past as fast as it could, which was about as fast as an old person could run, the way Charlie saw it. He lowered the M240 machine gun and surveyed the scene.

"That was it," Tommy said beside him, "that was the last of 'em!"

"For the here and now," Sammy said, "for the here and now."

No one said anything to that, for they all knew it was true, that at any moment reinforcements could begin to arrive, Grays armed with more than just their minds, with flash guns. For the moment, however, all that was in front of the two teams of humans were dozens of dead aliens, most lying in pools of their own greenish-blood and in many cases piles of shot-off alien body parts.

The platform was secure.

29 – THE HUB DOORS

Dulce Port (Level 1)
Thursday, May 24, 1979

"Shit!"

Turn shot his gaze forward, toward the X-22's cockpit and Captain Mark Richards seated in the pilot's seat.

"Shit!" Mark said again, this time slamming his hands down on the controls.

"What is it?" This time Turn was up beside him, a simple step with his cybernetic legs really all it took to clear the space separating them.

"HUB doors," Mark said, pointing out the cockpit window, "they're closing."

"But Aaron and his men from the helicopter made it inside!"

Mark shook his head at Turn's words. "Even though they got in there and got that sonic switched off and the holograms down, the hydraulics on all the door systems must still be working."

"So what can we do?" Turn bit his lip and stared at the HUB doors, now with just a sliver between them. They were huge things, two thick slabs of steel towering a good fifteen feet high and each as wide as the front of a barn. They were thick too, not as thick as blast doors meant to protect against a nuclear attack, but thick enough that once they were closed, no one was getting through.

"What the hell *can* we do?" Mark said, his hand slamming down on the cockpit controls once again, his frustration plain. "What the hell can we do?"

~~~

Inside the command facility where the base's controls and sonic killing system had been turned off, Command Sergeant Major Aaron Haney was thinking much the same thing.

"Hells bells!" he said, popping the clip from one of his Uzis and slamming it right back in again.

"What are we gonna do, sir?" Sergeant Paul Carson said, that calm voice and demeanor of his causing Aaron to frown at his own outburst.

"We're gonna get to those doors and get them the hell open, that's what we're gonna do!" Jerry said, then looked over at Aaron. "Isn't that right, sir?"

Aaron frowned again. The whole plan was going to hell, or at least changing rapidly. Already the HUB doors were nearly closed, and unless they acted in the next few seconds, they would be.

"We've got to get some explosives on those doors – pronto!"

"Comin' right up, sarge," Lewie said, then immediately began digging into the bulging pouches along his belt and in his jacket. Within moments he had several pieces of C4 explosives laid out on the table in front of them.

"Good," Aaron said, nodding at the explosives, "that'll get the job done, now we'll need two men to plant it, one on each of those doors."

"Well I'm going – they're my damn explosives!" Lewie said with a laugh, and just as the HUB doors slammed shut out in the greater port hangar. The men turned about and it was as if a collective sigh overtook them.

"And I'm going to," Jerry said next.

"Whoa," Paul said, holding up his hand, "if both of you go alone then you'll have no protection against the Gray's mind attacks."

"He's right," Johnny said, "once those Grays see you two moving out they'll open up with everything they've got in their heads – you won't stand a chance."

"Ha!" Lewie laughed. "We don't stand a chance as it is – how the hell we gonna get across thirty yards of hangar, aliens all about, and not get hit with something?"

"Because we'll have your asses, that's why," Aaron said, slamming that ammo clip into his gun again.

Paul nodded. "Then let's stop talking and start moving."

The men looked at one another again, each meeting their teammates' eyes. This was it, when battles hinged on single decisions and the willpower and bravery of but a few stood to affect the many, this was the moment.

The two men moved to the door.

~~~

"There!" Turn nearly shouted, his arm shooting out toward the cockpit window, nearly hitting the thing.

"I see them," Mark said back, and the two quieted down as they watched the two men – Paul Carson and Lewie Yates by the look of them – move out of the command facility door and then start to edge along the side of the building.

"They're going for the doors!" Andy shouted.

"No shit, Sherlock!" Billy said beside him, and with a good hit upside the head for good measure.

"Look!" Mark shouted, his finger going up this time.

The other men looked, then their eyes went wide.

~~~

"Run!" Paul shouted, but he knew it was too late. He and Lewie had only gone a dozen feet from the command facility and already the Grays were locking-in on them, and beginning to fire their flash guns.

Lewie didn't have to be told twice. He gripped his machine gun all the tighter and started moving, giving sideways shots toward the small clutch of Grays hiding out behind the huge UFO on their left.

"Go!" Paul shouted again, but at the same time he was doing his best to stay within ten feet or so of Lewie, enough to ensure the Grays couldn't use any mental attacks against him. If that happened, he knew, Lewie wouldn't stand a chance.

Lewie gritted his teeth and said 'the hell with it.' He put his machine gun up, began running, and began firing right at the side of the large UFO, expecting Grays to be there at any moment. Sure enough, there they were, a small bunch of them, just waiting to do their mental attacks.

"Take cover by the fighter craft!" Paul called out from behind, and Lewie hoped it was close enough still that the Grays couldn't get a beat on him. They were into the base now, rushing up to the main doors, and he expected they were damn mad about that, damn mad indeed. Watching a stream of his bullets rip into the aliens, shearing off their weak and frail arms before cutting into their bodies and heads, Lewie backed-off and started back toward the fighter craft lined-up on the other side of the floor from the large UFO. At the same time he shouldered the AR-15 machine gun and grabbed hold of his twin Colt .45s.

"Let's get down over here and pick 'em off," Paul said, already squatting down beside one craft.

The things were nothing more than hovering, black triangles by the look of it to Lewie, but they'd provide cover just like Paul said. He rushed up to the one beside Paul and started to–

BOOM!

The blast – whatever it was – took the craft Lewie had been running to out completely, and a large chunk sheared off, striking him right in the left leg. It took the leg right off.

"You bastard!" Lewie shouted just after he was whipped up into the air and then slammed down onto the hard, cement floor of the port hangar, the wind still somehow in him. All thoughts for his safety or well-being gone, he put up one of his Colt's and started firing wildly, like he imagined Custer and his boys had done one hundred years earlier at Little Bighorn.

Paul looked back at him and started to get up.

"Get those doors!" Lewie shouted at him through gritted teeth, not even looking his way, but knowing nonetheless that the younger soldier was going to try to save him. "I'm done. Get the doors and—"

Paul watched in horror as one of the flashgun laser shots from the Grays connected solidly with Lewie. Literally in a flash he was vaporized, his outline faintly juxtaposed against the hangar like some ghost of a photograph, and then he was gone, a small pile of fine, black powder all that remained beside his two Colts.

Paul gritted his teeth, but suppressed the urge to yell out and start firing at the Grays that'd did it, wherever they were, which he had no idea. Instead he put his head down and got his feet under him again, then started moving toward the HUB doors, now just—

Paul never knew what hit him, never knew anything again. The blast from a flashgun took him in the back and he was puffed out of existence not even a fraction of a second later.

~~~

"Shit!" Mark did shout this time, but instead of slamming his hands down on the X-22's controls he started pressing buttons and turning knobs.

"What are you doing, sir?" Turn asked from beside him.

"Blowing those fucking doors, what do you think?"

The tone in the younger Richards' voice told Turn not to say another word, for it was the same tone his grandmother used to use when she was busy in the kitchen back in the plantation house. Turn had learned real quick what that tone meant.

"What the hell are we—"

"Sit down and shut the hell up!" Mark shouted, his finger shooting out to point back at Billy. Billy's eyes went wide and he started backing away, like you would from an angry bear, slowly and without taking your eyes from the offending creature. Billy, Turn thought, *had* never learned what that tone meant.

"Here goes," Mark said under his breath, quiet enough for the two in the back to not hear, but loud enough for Turn to make out. With the final flip of a button the X-22's thrusters fired back to life and Mark 'rolled' her forward – that was the only way Turn could describe it – and they came to rest a good dozen yards *past* the command facility.

"Sir, don't you think we're getting too close to fire any–"

"Now!" Mark shouted to no one but himself, cutting off Turn's concerns in the process.

He hit the button on the side of the hand-held steering controls that fired the X-22's Hellfire missiles. Two shot forward, right toward the blast doors…both just forty yards away and well within the blast radius of the Hellfires. The X-22 was engulfed in flames.

30 – CAT-4

Dulce Platform (Level 7)
Thursday, May 24, 1979

There was a slight whistling sound and the eight men from CAT-1 and CAT-2 turned around quickly.

"Here's Colonel Donlon and CAT-4," Charlie said, lowering his M240 machine gun.

"Good," Tommy laughed, "I was gettin' mighty tired of standing around and countin' the dead bodies."

Charlie frowned at the young super soldier, but said nothing, and a few moments later the tube train carrying the four men of CAT-4 pulled into the platform.

"Goddamn!" Major Fred Sayer said, the first one out the tube train's doors as they swished open.

"You couldn't leave *any* for us?" David said, that perpetual frown of his turned on full blast at the moment.

"Oh, you'll get your share," Lieutenant Colonel Emil Wiseman said, his tobacco pipe clamped tightly between his teeth as usual.

"There'll be plenty more coming," Walter said as he came up to the train next, Major Jake Zates right on his heels. "Once the rest of the Grays in the secret bases around the US find out what's happening, they'll start sending in their security teams."

"And that's when we'll cut them down to bits," Donlon said. "There won't be a train stopping on this platform that doesn't see each and every occupant gunned-down in a manner of seconds when those tube train doors open."

"I hope so," Charlie said.

Donlon nodded at him, then looked around at the other eleven men.

103

"Alright, Charlie and Walter – get your teams moving out of this train terminal and starting up through the levels. By this time Richards and CAT-3 should have secured the entry port topside."

"Sonic's off," Walter said as he looked around at the ceiling above them, "or we'd be dead right now."

"And if it isn't we'll just have to take our chances," Donlon said.

Charlie nodded and stuck his hand out.

"Good luck, Roger" he said, and Donlon shook it. The rest of the men began to shake hands, and then CAT-1 and CAT-2 started walking down the platform, gingerly stepping over and around the numerous dead Grays littering the floor around them.

"Well, here we are, alone and in the depths of hell and just waitin' to die," Fred said when the last of the other teams' men vanished around the bend in the platform, where the tube train tracks kept shooting off into oblivion but the walkway turned left.

"I'm sure gonna take my fair share of aliens with me," Robbie laughed.

"Easy for you to say," David said as he turned on that frown full-blast, "you're a super soldier – you'll probably be the last to die."

"Can that nonsense," Donlon said, his words biting through the air. "Any minute now and another train's gonna come down those tracks, one most likely packed to the gills with Grays, or worse, their Reptilian allies."

"Reptilians?" Fred said. "No one said shit about those."

"Yeah, what–"

"You'll find out soon enough…although let's hope not." Roger rubbed at his forehead and bit his lip. "Just remember, if they move, you can kill 'em."

"Shouldn't these trains stop 'em?" David asked.

"They should, but–"

Roger's words were cutoff as the first train on the left side of the platform let out a blast of compressed air and then started to inch forward.

"What the hell!" Robbie shouted.

"Damn!" Donlon said, and started to rush down the platform.

"What's going on!" Fred shouted after him. He and the other two men took one look at each other and quickly started running after their commander.

"Damn Grays at one of the other bases figured out what's going on and is recalling the train."

"Recalling, what–"

"They're sending an electronic signal to the train to begin moving to the next station," Donlon yelled, still running down the platform, "that way they can get their trains right up to the platform, jumping out to kill us when the doors open."

"Well can't we just stop those trains from leaving!" David yelled up at him, his frown disappearing as the gravity of the situation made itself clear.

"What do you think I'm doing!" Roger yelled back, his frustration plain. A moment later he reached what he'd been running to, a small control station set up on the edge of the platform, right up against the wall that eventually turned into the bend leading to the stairs the other teams had just gone up. It wasn't much, just a waist-height counter-like-desk, a few control terminals to adjust incoming and outgoing trains, and more buttons and lights than any of the four men had an idea about.

"What is all this!" Fred yelled when all four men were within the confines of the small area, and just as the tube train that Charlie and CAT-1 had taken in sped pat them and vanished down the dark tunnel, past the last of the platform wall. The whistling sound started up just as soon as it'd gone, and the men looked back to see the train they'd come in on start to power up and begin moving as well.

"We've got to stop those trains from pulling out!" Donlon shouted as he started fiddling with the controls. "If we can't create a bottleneck at the end of the platform then we'll be overrun in no time."

"Well then how do we get it stopped!" Robbie yelled.

"I don't know!" Donlon yelled back. The men were frantically twisting knobs, hitting buttons, and pounding down on the lighted controls. Nothing seemed to work.

"Ah…fuck it!" David said, and brought his AR-15 up, the one with the grenade launcher attached.

"Wait, we need–"

Thunk, the grenade went as David pulled the trigger, then a moment later, BOOM! The tube train they'd rode in on was hit directly in the middle, the whole section blasted into twisted metal. The train lurched and then jumped the tracks and crashed into the side of the tube tunnel, it's progress stopped, and so too that of any train trying to come in behind it – that section of track was closed.

"Ha!" Fred laughed. "That might not be what we wanted, but it sure got the job done. Now we just…"

Fred trailed-off as a faint whistling sound could be heard, coming from behind them. The men turned about and looked down the tube tunnels from whence they'd come. There, rushing up at a breakneck speed, was the light of a tube train.

~~~

Walter ran forward, fired three shots from his AR15, ran forward a bit more, then fired another three shots. In less than four seconds he'd taken out four Grays and was running upon another pocket.

BOOM!

Not even wasting time to slow down as he approached the next turn in the long, tunnel-like hallways, he just grabbed one of the grenades at his waist, flicked the pin with his thumb, and threw it on ahead of him up around the bend. Sure enough, there'd been three Grays standing there, although it was hard to tell with the body parts laying about and the smoke rising from the charred and blackened pavement. He did notice one flashgun as he ran past, and his frown increased.

After heading off the platform the men of CAT-1 and CAT-2 had found the hallway, though there were numerous doors branching off. Most were rest areas and storage rooms, Walter knew from his time in the base years earlier, but the men couldn't risk leaving any aliens at their back, or at the back of the men of CAT-4 still on the tube train station platform, so the men were checking them. There were a few Grays here and there, but for the most part, they were empty. And without glancing back at all, Walter had no idea he'd outpaced the other men by several hundred feet.

Rounding the next bend brought him to a fork in the tunnel, one he knew about and had been expecting. Straight ahead there was a ramp that led up to the more open area of Nightmare Hall and the Hall of Horrors, two areas the men had been briefed on, and two he knew were going to be a shock to any who'd not seen them before. He glanced ahead, to the two tunnels leading the other way, and–

BOOM!

A blast of some sort hit the wall and he went down, a ringing in his ears. Coming to quickly, he stuck his machine gun out into the tunnel and fired off several short bursts, then stuck it the other way and fired a few more.

"You alright?"

It was Emil's voice, by the sound of it.

BOOM!

Another blast hit the wall just above Walter's head, and another round of loose cement pellets rained down upon him.

"Fine, just fine!" Walter said through clenched teeth while sticking his gun out to fire some more.

"We've got to get past this crossroads," Emil said, a few other men coming up behind him by the sound of it.

"Ready?" Walter said.

He didn't wait for an answer, just stuck his gun out and fired again. Emil knew the tone and the cue of his commander, and rushed forth through the gap in the tunnels, making it through the ten feet to the other side.

BOOM!

Another blast came, and again Walter was showered.

"Bastards!" he yelled, then gritted his teeth and yelled again to whatever men were behind him. "Go, go, go!"

The men rushed past as he fired.

~~~

Charlie came to a stop and put his hands on his knees. "I didn't think there'd be so much damn running!"

"You didn't think we'd be using the elevators, did you?" Tommy laughed, turning about to run backward for a minute and laugh at the overweight colonel. Already they'd run down quite the long hallway and then up a ramp. They were just nearing a larger, more open area by the looks of it.

"Keep your guard up," John said to him.

"Damn, that scowl alone'll scare away the first Grays that are dumb enough to come at us," Sammy said with a laugh, nodding at John's face for the others to see.

"If we don't die of exhaustion first," Charlie said. He'd started running again after the quick breather and now the four men of CAT-1 were nearing the top of the circular vehicle ramp, the one that led up from the lowest level of Dulce Base – Level 7 where the tube trains came in from the various bases around the world – up to Level 6. So far the four men hadn't once uttered what they expected to find there, mainly because they didn't want to think on it.

Behind them a good a good hundred yards or so – if you could measure distance like that going up a circular ramp (Charlie had told them to leave exactly two minutes after they did) – was CAT-2. Charlie had been adamant, and the Dutchman back at Blue Lake too, that the teams stagger their arrival on the next level up, just in case there was some kind of ambush and one team was wiped out. Charlie frowned as he thought back on that briefing over their weeks of training, for it was now they that were the team most likely to die a sudden and fiery death.

"There it is," Tommy said, and Charlie looked up to what the young and cocky super soldier was nodding at. Sure enough, there was the opening to the next level.

"They'll be up there," Sammy said, his Mossberg 590 shotgun gripped tightly in his hands, "they'll be up there, and they'll be ready."

"We don't know that," John said.

"The power's been cut and the security systems are down – I'm sure they know."

Sammy looked over at Charlie and frowned, but had to admit the older corporal was right. They ran on the last few yards and then the sloping floor evened-out and they were there.

"Holy…mother of God," Sammy said as he saw the level first. There before them were row upon row of large, glass vats, each containing ungodly horrors, atrocities, monstrosities…his fellow man.

Tommy leaned over and began to retch.

"No time for that," Charlie said, gritting his teeth and fighting the urge to do the same, "we've got a dish of cold revenge to serve up."

He gripped his twin colts a bit tighter and was just about to start forward when footfalls from behind forced his attention back. Coming up fast was Bobbie and two others from CAT-2. Charlie made to signal and point out what was ahead, but then he remembered that Bobbie had seen it all before, being a super soldier, and probably knew–

Charlie's train of thought was stopped completely when Bobbie rushed up to and then past him and his team members.

"Here," he called out, rushing up to what looked like a regular wall, but which Charlie now realized was a very-well-concealed doorway. Walter jiggled the handle, found it open, and pushed on inside. There were five Grays gathered around the control stations, but Bobbie's eyes lit on just one, the one standing a good four to five feet taller than the others, and pointing a flashgun his way.

ZAP!

The Gray fired at the same instant Bobbie dove from the doorway, his body angled so he'd fall on his side, something that allowed him to pull up the Heckler & Koch and fire off a short burst while flying through the air.

OOMPH!

Bobbie hit the cement floor of the security station hard and right on his shoulder.

POP!

"Aaahhh!" he grunted through clenched teeth, his shoulder either breaking or popping out of its joint. His right arm now useless, he began transferring the machine gun to his left hand, all the while watching the four Grays trying to sort themselves out (the tallest one was now lying dead with three bullet holes in its large forehead).

"Hey!"

Both Bobbie's and the Grays' eyes all shot over to the door, where Charlie was just coming in, one of his two Colt .45s leading the way. Bobbie saw a slight smile come to Charlie's face, then he unleashed whatever pent-up frustrations he had.

BANG! BANG! BANG! BANG!

Bobbie could only stare wide-eyed as Charlie fired off the four shots, western-style with his palm running over the hammer after each shot. A few seconds later the floor was littered with four more Grays and Bobbie knew that Clint Eastwood didn't have shit on Chargin' Charlie!

"Shewww!" John whistled, coming into the room next, Emil and then Jake from Bobbie's CAT-2 following close on his heels. He smiled and was about to crack a joke – even with Bobbie still on the ground and favoring his shoulder – when something on one of the numerous TV monitors in the room caught his attention.

"Holy shit!"

Bobbie turned his attention and quickly went up to the monitor John was looking at, just as Tommy and Sammy came into the small security facility next. There, in cages and spread all out on what looked to be a massive open floor area, were human females, most crying piteously for help by the look of it, though there was no sound coming from the monitors.

"So many..." Tommy said, walking up to the monitors, his eyes wide. "There were never supposed to be so many..."

"What is he talking about?" Bobbie asked, coming up to the two. Charlie turned about quickly and gave him a strange look.

"How's that shoulder?"

Bobbie gave him a hard look, then slammed his shoulder into a pair of low-level cabinets hanging from the ceiling.

POP!

"Aaahhh!"

"*Shit!*"

Charlie continued shaking his head after the curse, once again surprised by the sheer strength, and outright stupidity, of Bobbie and the rest of the super soldiers. For his part, Bobbie just laughed and shrugged, though it was clear he was in pain.

"Fixed now," was all he said as some tobacco juice drooled from one corner of his mouth, then pointed at the monitors. "So what gives?"

"What gives is that—"

"We were had," Walter said, and the men turned to see their commander coming into the room. It was clear he'd been in some fire fights, as one side of his face was covered in the greenish-goo that was either the Gray's blood or the liquid they bathed in...maybe both. He took one look at the monitors then shook his head. "This isn't just a search and destroy mission anymore, gentlemen – it's a rescue mission."

"A rescue..." Charlie scoffed, then just trailed off, shaking his head.

Walter nodded. "A rescue mission." He nodded at the monitors, as if that should make it all obvious.

"What...what is it...Walter?" he asked after he'd threw up his arms, for there were two different scenes, depending on which monitors you looked at, which side of the room you could handle. One held the women, the other....

"Hell," Emil said, "Hell – that's all I can think."

"Not Hell, but close," Tommy said, "The Hall of Horrors."

On the monitors ahead of them it was clear that there were two main areas. The one on the right side of the room, stretching for as far as they eye could see by the look of it, held row upon row of large, glass vats. They looked like huge, monstrous fish tanks, though instead of clear water, each was filled with some kind of greenish…goo, was all anyone could really describe it as. But it was what was floating in those vats that really set the men's nerves on edge.

There were humans, rows and rows of them, most not moving, most looking dead. Several of the vats had Grays in them, some moving about, treading water if you will, others looking about as dead as the things that were floating with them. And those things were often human arms, legs, internal organs, cow parts, and even other animal parts and appendages. Walter took it all in and then thought he'd have to turn about and empty his dinner onto the concrete floor of the level ramp.

"Easy,' Emil said, coming up to him, "you've been here before, remember?"

"Yeah, and I sure the hell don't remember this."

"This wasn't here back in '75?" Jake asked.

"Hell no it wasn't!" Walter said. "I mean, we knew they were doing genetic testing, we knew about the stuff the Dutchman and Gus and all the rest told us about…but this," he shook his head and scoffed, "this is just…"

"It's Hell," Emil said again, his pipe moving about nervously, "now let's destroy it."

"And what about the other side?" Bobbie said, his teeth gritted but his pain looking under control.

"That's Nightmare Hall," Walter said with barely a pause, "that's where the testing's always traditionally gone on, where the abductees wound up."

"Abductees?" Charlie said. "What the hell?"

"It was supposed to be less than a hundred at first, then it became hundreds." Walter shook his head. "That was in '75…who knows how many are there now."

"Over 30,000 captives on that one level alone," John said, and everyone spun around to see the helmeted major looking down at some kind of clipboard…though one that looked to have a small TV screen in it.

"What's that?" Tommy said coming up, but John just swatted him away.

"Some kind of hand-held computer, what's it look like?"

"Hand-held *computer*?" Bobbie laughed, but both Walter and Charlie were already moving past the other men to get a look at it, and the data it held.

"God, it's in English and it's talking about places like the 'testing facilities' and 'pleasure centers' and—"

"Where are they?" Walter said, and from his tone it was clear he was ready to rip some heads off, hopefully Grays'.

John shook his head, the overlarge helmet swaying back and forth. "Says they're in over sixty different locations…and there's more than 4,500 of 'em."

"Pleasure centers?" Emil said with disgust, his tongue sticking out, something that almost caused his pipe to fall on the floor…almost.

The room grew quiet, and everyone looked to Walter, for there were only two commanders among them, and he was the only to have seen this area before. He frowned, then gestured down to the satellite phone strapped to Jake's leg.

"We're calling this in to headquarters," he said, "the mission has changed."

PART IV
31 – A CHANGE OF ORDERS

Kirtland Air Force Base – Albuquerque, New Mexico
Thursday, May 24, 1979

General Harry Anderholt sat behind his large mahogany desk and couldn't stop tapping his fingers. He was nervous, out of sorts, and on edge. Right now the four CAT teams were in Dulce – Ellis's son hitting the ground level, two teams fighting up to the top, and one team holding the base against enemy intrusion. Besides that there was the Fast Action Team of astronauts and engineers, plus the cleanup team held in reserve. It should be enough, he kept telling himself, but then why were those damn fingers of his tapping incessantly? Anderholt frowned at the thought and stopped tapping them, and just then the phone rang. He picked it up, unknowingly tapping his fingers all the while.

"Anderholt," he said in a gruff voice.

"Sir, we've had developments," the Dutchman's voice came to him over the line.

"Shoot," Anderholt said. If there was one word to portray multiple feelings and answers and states of mind, General Harry Anderholt was going to use it.

"CAT-2 just reached Level 7…Nightmare Hall." There was a slight pause and an audible sigh and Anderholt pictured Ellis shaking his head and rubbing at his brow back at Blue Lake. "Sir, there are thousands of them, thousands of abductees…the vast majority of them women." He paused. "The men found a report saying there were 30,000 females alone."

Anderholt took in a deep breath. He was afraid of this.

"That many, huh? And how many of them are in the shape to move."

Once again it was a kind of loaded question, one with a double-meaning, and Ellis immediately took it both ways.

"The ones that aren't too far gone genetically are mostly just drugged-up...at least by what Captain Leathers is reporting," Ellis said. "Overall, I'd say eighty to ninety percent of the victims are salvageable."

"Salvageable," Anderholt repeated with a laugh, "Ellis, they're—"

"They *were* human, at least in the case of most of them," Ellis shot back quickly, cutting of the general's words. He didn't' like challenging authority, yet it was something he did on an almost weekly basis.

"And what are they now?" Anderholt shot right back.

There was a tense silence on the line as the two men stood their ground. Finally Anderholt broke it with a sigh.

"Listen, Ellis – this wasn't part of the plan."

"The plans have changed sir, doesn't this prove it."

"So what do you want to do...save them all?"

"I want to give it the ol' college try, sir?"

Oh, Hell's bells, Anderholt thought, but said, "it's your show, Ellis, and your boy is running it on the ground."

"Not anymore, sir – I'm going in."

Anderholt was about to protest, but the other end of the line went dead.

32 – THE PLATFORM

Dulce Platform (Level 7)
Thursday, May 24, 1979

"Aaahhh!" First Lieutenant Robbie Biscaye yelled, bringing the two Ingram MAC-10s up and out so they were balanced on his hips. Looking on from a few feet away, Major Fred Sayer could have sworn that the four Grays that'd been rushing toward Robbie had their huge, black eyes go just a bit wider. There was really no way to tell. A split-second later Robbie pulled the triggers, and besides the 'buzzing' sound, sixty bullets shot out as if they were a saw cutting through air. They tore into the Grays, slicing through the frail bodies like they were twigs in a forest. The bodies were shot apart and arms and torsos and heads and necks all hung suspended in the air for a brief moment before falling haphazardly to the floor, greenish-goo everywhere.

"Ha!" David shouted from nearby. "That was good, but check this out!"

David waited until at least one of his team members' eyes was on him, then turned his attention back to the small pocket of Grays huddling beside the ruined tube train that he'd already twisted to hell with the earlier grenade launcher blast. He gripped the AR-15 tightly, then pulled the trigger to the China Lake grenade launcher positioned on top. A 40x46mm grenade shot out at 249 feet per second and, making David's heart skip a beat in delight, two of the Grays just happened to turn to look at the flying projectile right before it reached them.

BOOM!

The grenade hit directly in front of the Grays, and since they were standing right in the midst of the ruined tube train, each of the creatures was ripped apart as the blast sent them flying into the sharp and twisted metal still sticking out at all angles. Another black char-mark was left on the

114

tracks and part of the platform and much of the wall and once again, there were alien body parts lying everywhere.

"Heh," David laughed, "how you like them apples!"

Robbie frowned, not liking them much at all, but liking being shown-up even less. Of course the situation they were in really took the cake when it came to things he didn't like. He may have been the only super soldier on this small four-man team down in the bowels of Dulce, but he sure felt like an insignificant crumb. A lot of that had to do with the Reptilians.

The creatures had first arrived just a few seconds before, on one of the many trains that kept rushing to Dulce's underground platform…from wherever the hell they were coming from. It didn't matter much, Robbie knew, just stopping the damn things. The only consolation was that while the Grays were capable of mind attacks, the Reptilians weren't – that'd been drummed into all the super soldiers back when they'd first trained to become the elite special forces alien killers…and protectors. For no matter how many of the vile creatures, or the equally-vile Grays (for Robbie wasn't one to discriminate, growing up poor in the South had taught him that) came at the men, he knew that his primary responsibility was protecting the men around him…and that something he could do just by being there.

"Here's another one!" Donlon yelled out, breaking Robbie from his thoughts for a moment. The four men looked over, and sure enough, there was another gaggle of Reptilians coming up the tube train tracks, the sheer number of stopped trains now blocking the platform ensuring that any additional alien security forces sent in to stop the attacking human teams would have to hoof it down the tunnels, oh, probably a good 300 feet by now at the least, most of them figured. Already there were more than a dozen trains on either side of the platform, and who knew how many further back where the darkness became too much for them to see.

Robbie bit his lip and swallowed a curse, for no matter how many invectives he hurled, the damn aliens would keep coming. He gripped the twin Ingram MAC-10 submachine guns tightly before pulling the triggers. Immediately .45 caliber ACP Parabellum bullets spit out of the 146 mm barrels, and at the astonishing rate of 1,146 rounds per minute. He arced the two guns in two steady streams, back and forth, sending wave upon wave of bullets out.

CLICK!

David looked over at Robbie, who frowned.

"Damn things only get thirty to a clip!"

David scoffed and shook his head and looked back to where the Reptilians were still charging down the tunnel, just then reaching the platform and beginning to hoist themselves up. He patted the 40mm pump-action China Lake grenade launcher at his side and smiled. "Time for the big dog to eat."

He pulled the trigger and the grenade launcher spat out a single grenade right into the midst of the oncoming Reptilians, blowing them to bits and pieces every which way. The creatures were something else entirely. They wore no clothes, just a sort of utility belt that held some of its weapons, and had large claw-like talons on their dinosaur-like feet. Their yellow, slit-serpentine eyes shone out of those hideous scaled-bodies as they jumped forth, a God-awful hissing sound shooting from their mouths.

David laughed and pulled the trigger again, sending another round out and right where the first had landed. As he'd expected, there'd been another five to six Reptilians rushing right through there, expecting the route to now be clear. He pulled the trigger a third time, sending the gun's final grenade, but this time only two of the creatures were taken out.

"That's the big dog!" he growled at Robbie before laughing and quickly sticking the shotgun-like grenade launcher in it's holder at his thigh before pulling out his AR15 assault rifle.

"Now it's time for dessert!" Robbie shouted back, his twin MAC-10s loaded once again. Another wave of sixty bullets tore into the oncoming line of Reptilians, but on they came.

"Shit," Fred muttered, seeing yet another pocket of Reptilians coming down the opposite track. He put up his Colt AR15 Commando, the same assault carbine each of the men had in addition to whatever 'toys' they'd carried along, and the gun spat out several short bursts of small caliber rounds at a rate of 750 rounds per minute. A few Reptilians fell to the bullets, but the onrush continued.

"They'll overrun us," he said, lowering the gun. Around him the men of CAT-4 frowned, and started to wonder how much time they had.

33 – NIGHTMARE HALL

Nightmare Hall (Level 6)
Thursday, May 24, 1979

Jake rushed forward, and then tried his best to skid to a halt. There before him was a man…a hideous, deformed man.

"Ugh…" he moaned, his head whipping down to catch sight of Jake, the movement catching his eye. Jake saw those eyes go wide, as if he couldn't believe what he was seeing.

Jake couldn't believe what he was seeing, either. The man was stationed on some kind of large platform, at least ten feet up off the ground. It had to be that tall for the man's testicles were as tall as small trees, and looked like large, overfilled balloons ready to burst. And between them, where Jake imagined the man's penis was, or at least some gross caricature of it, was what he could only describe as a milking machine, like he'd seen on some dairy farms growing up. The man was being milked for his sperm, his balls somehow modified to produce the stuff endlessly. Looking up into his eyes again, Jake didn't know if that meant he was in constant pleasure, or constant pain.

"Kill…me…" the man said, and a teardrop fell from his right eye, skimming across the black teardrop tattoo there.

Jake didn't have to be told twice. He raised his M16, took aim right at that small tattoo, and let off a huge burst of gunfire and a hideous yell, hoping to capture some of the man's anguish at what he'd been put through for the past…God only knew how many years.

Jake lowered the gun and saw that the man was dead, the aliens robbed of one of their 'cows.' He shook off the terrible thought and continued on, his boots drumming on the metal walkway as he ran.

Ahead was Walter, still rushing forth into the larger, open-area of

Nightmare Hall. He and Emil had gone ahead, expecting their super soldier Bobbie to be just behind. Thankfully both were just ahead and firing like madmen, oblivious to the detour off the beaten path the two men had taken.

After making the call to General Anderholt and then getting word that the mission had changed from one of search and destroy to one of rescue and run, Walter's demeanor had changed. It was as if he were fighting for something more, something that wasn't part of the regular agenda.

Jake rushed forward, actually getting ahead of Bobbie, but not enough that he was going to worry about it. His adrenaline was pumping, his heart beating fast – safety was the last thing on his mind.

He rounded the bend and the ramp began to level off, the next level-up of the base coming right up before them. Jake, Walter, Bobbie and Emil all made it up, shoes pounding on the pavement, that the only sound as they raced higher, and then reached the top and the opening. It was there that Jake finally stopped and stood, his eyes wide and mouth agape. The TV monitors of the security facility were one thing, but seeing Nightmare Hall in person was quite another. It was the endless screaming and crying and wailing that hit them hardest of all.

"God, won't they stop?" he said, his face scrunched up as he tried to block out the sound with his hands over his ears. It did little good.

"They will when we get them out of here," Walter said, "now this is what we're gonna do." The other three men gathered closer as ahead of them the cages of women – nearly all that they saw were women, all naked, though there were a few that looked like men – and Walter laid it out. "We've gotta stay close, so I want Bobbie walking down that main hallway there," he pointed, and the blackness hundreds of feet ahead swallowed up wherever it went, "and Emil, I want you and Jake opening those cages on either side."

Emil nodded. "And you, Walt?"

"I'll take the rear, hitting anything that could come up behind."

"Think they can make it?" Bobbie said, nodding at the caged women.

Walter shook his head. "Looks like many can move, but how far they'll get or where they'll go..."

"Let's just get to it," Jake said, and the others nodded.

Bobbie moved ahead first, his Heckler & Koch machine gun held out before him, but there were no Grays to be seen. On either side of him Emil and Jake quickly opened the many cages. The things were kennels, really, about the size you'd find in an animal shelter, though in some spots they were much smaller, and stacked, with the women crammed into them, hardly any room to move. It was they that were the most far gone. With the larger kennels the women rushed out. From behind Jake and Emil, Walter had to call to them to move down the hallway they'd come from, to not cling to the men. It was hard, as many were crying with terror, most wailing that they'd be killed at any moment.

"Run down the hall!" Walter shouted at them. "You'll be alright – there are men there waiting for you."

He wasn't sure it was true, but what else was he supposed to say? General Anderholt had assured him new teams would be mobilized, and that the women just had to make it to the tube station platform where CAT-4 was. He hoped that would truly be enough, and that the suffering and anguish of these women could end.

Most were little more than college-aged women, some even teens or adolescents. All were beautiful and nearly all were blonde. Most were short as well, and Walter couldn't help but think of his two daughters back home in Tucson, as well as what awful things the Grays would do to them if they were here in place of some of these women. At one point one of the more held-together of the many women – they were all beginning to blend together as the team progressed down the seemingly endless-hallway unmolested – came up to him and grabbed his shoulder.

"I've been here for two months, I've been raped everyday and I've had two…miscarriages of some sort, thought how that'd be possible in that amount of time, don't ask me."

Walter just nodded, hoping she'd run off like the rest. Already there'd been thousands.

"You've got to listen to me, I–"

Walter turned about to scold her, tell her to run along to the train platform. He was just in time to see her head explode like a melon that'd been struck with a mallet. His eyes went wide and saw a Gray standing behind them, women screaming and rushing past it as it aimed its flashgun right at his head.

"Down!" Walter yelled as the Gray fired, and dropped to the floor.

Behind him Bobbie was just turning about when the flashgun blast hit him. Jake was looking right at him and saw him wink out of existence in a flash of light, the kind that allowed you to see every bone in the person's body. It was a fraction of a second and then there was just a pile of soot on the concrete floor. A chill came over Jake and he felt his mouth opening to scream. He turned about to do so and saw a sight almost as fearful – Emil with his eyes in a rage, teeth clenched, and Heckler & Koch MP5 submachine gun shouldered.

BAM! BAM! BAM! BAM! BAM! BAM!

It was on single-shot for some reason, but each of those shots tore into the Gray's head and made any facial features that may have set it apart from its brethren little more than a meaty pulp.

"Bobbie!" Jake yelled.

"He's dead," Walter said evenly and without emotion, getting up now that no other Grays looked to be about. The tide of women was also receding, though their screams were not.

"No shit," Emil said in reply, "and that's what we'll be here real quick if we don't get another super soldier. Or were you planning on developing some kind of mind-attack blocking capability real quick here, huh?"

Walter looked at the hardheaded Lieutenant Colonel, that ever-present pipe stuck in his mouth dangling as annoyingly as usual, and then to Major Jake Zates. He frowned.

"I don't know how to say this, boys, but I'm heading in to save as many of these women as I can."

Emil moved the pipe from one side of his mouth to the other, shaking his head all the while, while Jake just looked like he was one more second closer to losing his mind from fear. Walter laughed.

"Shit, you men get back to that tube train platform and give Donlon and his boys on CAT-4 some support, and that's an order."

"Yes, sir," Jake said, the screaming of the still-caged women plus the loss of their super soldier nearly fraying the last of his nerves. It was clear to Walter that he'd do anything to get out of there, and therefore was more of a risk to them than a benefit, at least until he got a hold of himself, and he sure the hell wasn't going to be doing that on the edge of Nightmare Hall. Emil was a bit harder to convince.

"You know if you head any further in there you won't be heading back out," he said, the pipe clamped tightly.

"CAT-2 is yours, Colonel," Walter said with a nod, then ran ahead into the darkness.

34 – THE HALL OF HORRORS

The Hall of Horrors (Level 5)
Thursday, May 24, 1979

The men of CAT-1 fought their way across the floor of the Hall of Horrors, shooting out any vats with Grays floating inside, and quite a few that had deformed and mutated humans as well. There was one with a man sporting octopus arms and a bewildered expression; another holding a woman with four heads, not all of them on top; and several with humans that were either totally are halfway-transformed into some kind of snake or serpent creature or…sometimes it was just hard to tell exactly *what* they were looking at. One thing was clear, however, and that was that the defense was growing stronger.

Sammy walked steadily forward, the Mossberg Model 590 shotgun held out confidently before him. Another Gray jumped forward, seemingly out of nowhere, and once again Sammy was sure he saw fear or surprise or something in those black orbs when he kept walking forward, when he raised the gun up slightly higher on his shoulder, when he finally pulled the trigger, often with a 'fuck you' thrown in for good measure. This time was no different, and the 12-gauge cartridge shot out the side of the gun as the bullet shot into the Gray's head and tore it apart, showering the walls and floor with that greenish-goo.

"Goddamn, Sammy!" Tommy shouted from behind. "That's nine of the bastards now!"

The words barely registered for Sammy, so intent was he on what lay ahead. The men were advancing steadily through the row upon rows of glass vats spaced evenly on the floor around them, the whole multiple-acre level being taken up by them. It was a ghastly sight, with Grays floating in the tanks, most oblivious to them, like they were under the effect of some strange drug, one that made them completely useless. Of course they weren't all useless, and as the men moved through the level, shooting nearly every vat they saw along the way – and especially those holding Grays or hopelessly mutated humans – quite a few of the aliens stirred themselves and made to attack. And oh how feeble and comical those attacks were! In most cases a Gray would be able to get itself up over the lip of the vat, perhaps thinking it could get some kind of mind attack off, but invariably they tried to fall back into the 'safety' of the greenish-goo when the attack somehow failed. And that's when the men of CAT-1 and CAT-2 opened up on them.

Beside Sammy, Major John Bingham brought up his AR-15 and sent a hail of machine gun bullets out at two more Grays that jumped out from behind some of the vats, two more of what Charlie was calling the 'base security forces.'

"Shit!" he shouted, his heart nearly skipping a beat at the sight of the things.

"Just stay close to Tommy and me," Sammy said as he loaded a few more shells into his shotgun, the others covering him with their guns pointed down the tunnels. "You stay close and their mind tricks won't do a damn thing."

"Won't do a damn thing but fool the hell out of 'em!" Tommy shouted back with a laugh. "Bastards can't even read our minds – they don't even know we're comin'!"

Charlie heard the words and frowned. *They will*, he thought, *God help us, they will.*

He held his M240 machine gun out with one hand and fired at any Gray that moved, and with the other he reached down to the special satellite radio at his waist. If he could just get one call off...one call to Blue Lake...

You'll never get a call off to Blue Lake, why on earth would you want to do such a thing?

Charlie looked up to see what beautiful face held the beautiful voice that just spoke to him, and he wasn't disappointed. There, in a pool of the bluest mountain lake water he'd ever seen, was the most beautiful woman he'd ever seen. Her hair was blond and flowed about her naked body slowly, the currents in the water moving the hair just so, obscuring all the best parts, leaving it all to Charlie's imagination.

Forget Blue Lake, Charlie – make love to me...now!

How could Charlie refuse? That was the thought going through his mind as he started forward, past the few trees blocking his path, and then as he took the last few steps to the lake shore and–

"Colonel!"

John's shout from back on the main pathway barely registered with Charlie, but Tommy running toward him as fast as he could did. One moment Charlie was reaching out to the beautiful woman in the lake that was reaching back to him, the next he was looking some kind of...thing.

"My...God," he managed as Tommy reached him and put his hand on his shoulder. It was some kind of human, or at least had been one, though now it's head had nothing more than one large eye under a head of blond hair. Their was a neck going down to a pair of shoulders, but then the torso trailed off into a amphibian-like tail, the arm-like appendages little different. Charlie bent over and started to feel sick.

"Don't get so far away from Sammy or I," Tommy said, and even through bouts of puking Charlie could detect the serious tone in the young corporal's voice, a rare thing indeed. After a moment he was fine. Without a word he let go of the machine gun so it dangled from his shoulder, pulled out the two Colt .45s at his waist, and unloaded each of them into the monstrosity staring back at them from behind the glass vat. Charlie liked to think the thing's eye went a little larger at the sight, and also that it's last thought was one of fear before his two revolvers put an end to it. He didn't want to think that it might have once been a young woman.

"Let's go," Tommy said, pulling his commander back to the main pathway or roadway that led through the seemingly endless room of tanks and vats and experimental pools.

"Damn," he shouted out between bursts from his M16 and the occasional launched grenade from the M203 mounted on top, indicating to Sammy and John that he was drawing near once again, "they just keep comin'!"

"No shit," John yelled from a short distance ahead on the road. His machine gun had jammed a short time before and now he was firing away with his two 9mm pistols.

"Just stay close," Sammy said.

"And keep moving," Charlie added.

The four men kept close and kept moving, the goo-filled vats all around them, blocking their view of what lay ahead, obfuscating where the end of the level was, and ensuring that the men would always be guessing, would never be knowing.

"If we can just get up past these last few vats there looks to be a straight path forward," Sammy said after they'd gone another few yards, and blown-out another few vats, "after that we should be—"

HISS!

It was like the sound a snake would make, one that was large and able to eat a man, by the sound of it. But it wasn't a snake, it was a Reptilian, an especially large one, and one that'd gotten into their midst without the men even knowing.

The creature had been atop the vats, running up from the side, out of view of both Combat Assault Teams. It'd leaped and hissed and that's when the men had looked up, just before the thing fell atop Sammy, its claws and its teeth working.

"Aaahhh!" Sammy yelled as the thing landed atop him then lunged forward with its scaled-snout, tearing into the soft flesh of the super solder's face.

"Shoot it!" Tommy yelled, bringing up his M16.

"No!" Charlie shouted beside him, and swatted the barrel of his gun away. "It's too close."

And it was. The alien from the Draco Constellation was lashing and tearing and shredding with those clawed hands it had, as well as rending with those razor-sharp clawed-feet. But at the same time Sammy was whirling around, spinning in circles as he frantically tried to throw the creature off him.

"Colonel...do something!" John yelled, his two 9mm desperately trying to find an opening.

"Ah, hell!" Charlie said, then whipped out one of the Colt .45s at his belt, just like the men would expect a gunslinger of the old West to do the same, and fired a hipshot right at the struggling pair.

The shot was true, and hit the Reptilian right in the back, eliciting a howl of displeasure and pain from the beast. It was enough to get its toothy-beak off of Sammy's face, and enough for Tommy to get a single shot to the head off with his machine gun. The Reptilian's head was thrown back and those slit-serpentine eyes of it seemed to flutter and then roll back before the creature's tight grip on Sammy faltered, then faded, and then dropped off altogether. The thing fell to the floor, dead.

"Aaahhh, aaahhhh, aaahhh!" Sammy screamed, his hands clasping his face, blood running out from between his fingers.

"Jesus," Charlie said, shaking his head at the sight, "if we don't—"

CRASH!

Charlie was thrown to the ground as something exploded in their midst, something so strong that all of the vats around them exploded and that pinkish goo went flying every which way. Charlie rolled over on the floor, broken vat glass crunching beneath him. His ears were ringing and things seemed to be moving in slow motion. His vision was blurred, but he looked out and could make out...Sammy, laying still and not moving on the floor, John...clutching his ears and...screaming, by the looks of it.

Tommy, where is Tommy? The thought came to Charlie as he realized Sammy was dead. That meant they had one super soldier, their only real line of defense against the Grays and their mental attacks. Where was...

No...God, no, Charlie thought, his vision beginning to clear, at least enough for him to see a few more feet, though he wished it hadn't. For there on the floor ten feet away was Tommy, a large shard of vat glass sticking from his head, his eyes staring out wide in death.

God help us, Charlie thought at the sight, *God help us!*

35 – PULL-OUT

Dulce Port (Level 1)
Thursday, May 24, 1979

"Get that fucking door open!" Captain Mark Richards shouted.

"Damn thing won't budge, sir!" Andy shouted back.

Mark sighed, then started moving forward. "Here, move out of the way."

He got his hands into the crack in the door and started pulling, Andy joining in from the other side.

"She's moving!" Turn and Billy both shouted.

"Ugh!" Mark and Andy both grunted at the same time, and the door came open.

There were no aliens around them now, the port area completely burned out, especially the charred and blackened area around the HUB doors.

"Damn, sir – you really blew the hell out of them!" Billy laughed.

Mark looked over at the charred doors as he hopped out of the bruised and battered X-22. They were completely gone, the two Hellfire rockets having obliterated them as much as three-feet-thick steel could be obliterated. The remnants hung their like two sad window shutters after a particularly bad storm.

"Cooked their gooses, too," Andy laughed. "There ain't an alien in sight!"

Mark looked around and saw he was right. The whole floor of the port was now clear, with just the red flashing security lights moving. Even the desert to the rear was visible to them, the wind kicking up small swirls of sand and dust. His attention was ripped back to the entry port when a clicking sound came. He and the others looked over to see the door to the command facility opening, Jerry gingerly sticking his head out the door.

126

"Jerry!" Billy shouted, and he smiled further when Aaron and Johnny came out next.

"Shit, we thought you guys were toast!" he said, throwing open the door, though keeping his machine gun up.

"It's clear…or at least that's what it looks like," Mark said to him as he started to walk from the X-22 and back across the floor. The others inside the command facility started to come out as well, and within moments the seven men were standing there, guns in hand, as they figured out the next move.

"Listen up, men," Mark said, "we could stand here and cry over spilled milk and recap what's happened so far, or we can just get our asses through those doors and blow as many more aliens to hell in the twenty-five minutes or so of this mission we've got left."

There were several cocked-eyebrows and slight smiles to that, but not a man said a word. Mark frowned.

"Fuck it – I'm going in, and if any of you want to follow, so be it."

He took off toward the HUB doors, or what was left of them. The others looked at one another, and then with an Oorah from Jerry, they fell in behind their commander.

~~~

On the other edge of the port floor, Eddie ran forward and ducked under the UFO, some kind of fighter craft, by the look of it.

"There's no one here!" Ronnie laughed behind him, walking fully upright, Stan at his side.

"You want to push those Grays?" Eddie scoffed. "Who knows how many could still be hiding in here."

"After the blast the Dutchman's son gave those doors?" Stan laughed. "C'mon, Eddie – get your head on straight."

Eddie frowned as the two astronaut-engineers reached him, but slowly stood up as well.

"So can you get 'er airborne?" Stan asked, thumping the UFO with his fist.

"If I can get 'er open," Eddie replied with a smile."

"Well, grab on right there," Ronnie said, pointing out some grooves under the craft's cockpit area.

The thing looked like a triangle with a small, glass-enclosed cockpit area nestled down into it's body, although it wasn't glass, but something else. Eddie had seen it at Los Alamos before and knew that they were working on creating something similar using the same alien technology, it was just that they weren't quite there yet. And the craft wasn't completely a mystery to him, either. It looked to be about the same make and mode – how else would you describe it, Eddie always explained to anyone that asked – and that meant he could fly it.

"One…two…three!" Eddie said, and together the three men pulled up, straining against the thing until the 'glass' top popped-open.

"Same one?" Ronnie asked once they'd caught their breath and rubbed their fingers, and as if reading his friend's thoughts.

Eddie nodded, biting his thumb as he stared at the thing and ran through the myriad combinations in his head. "Same one we've been testing since '56 and the Lake Oswego Incident."

Ronnie and Stan both nodded. No one needed to explain what the Lake Oswego Incident was.

"You sure this is really a good idea?" Stan asked next. "I mean, this wasn't part—"

"Watching Paul and Lewie die back there wasn't part of the plan either," Eddie shot back. Stan backed off, and Eddie saw that he'd come on too strong. "Listen, I can—"

"I know," Stan said, and clapped him on the shoulder.

"Get up there," Ronnie said next, and Eddie nodded before getting into the UFO. The men closed the UFO fighter craft's top and then Eddie started to work the controls.

"Back up," Stan said, pulling Ronnie back a bit.

The two men then stood back and stared as Eddie got the thing fired up. There was no sound, just a faint, reddish glow emanating from under it. Then, faster than a blink of an eye it seemed, the craft shot up three feet.

"Whoa!" both men said, and then the craft spun around and shot off into the desert night.

36 – CHANGING COURSE

Dulce Tunnels (Level 2)
Thursday, May 24, 1979

The men of CAT-3 ran on, over the large cement floor that was marked off with street lines. It was the main highway into and out of the base...for humans that is. Already they'd left the port area and blasted-out HUB doors way behind. The ceilings were now twenty-five feet above them and the first ramp leading down to Level 2 was just ahead. Mark hit it first, and didn't look back to see if any of his men had followed him, though all had. There was Andy and Billy keeping pace, though staying just at his heels. Behind them ran Aaron, Jerry and Johnny. And all six of the men were staying as close to Turn as they could. For Turn that was both a source of pride and one of frustration. It's true that he wanted to use his super soldier status to protect the men, but he also wanted to use his cybernetic legs to shoot ahead of them, clearing the way of all dangers. It was a noble thought, and also a stupid one. That's what he had to keep reminding himself as they ran on, his pencil-thin mustache beading with sweat more than usual.

BEEP-BEEP

The men stopped right at the same time Mark threw his hand up into the air in a fist, the sign for them to do so. He quickly reached down to the satellite radio in a leg pocket and got it out.

"Mark, orders have changed."

The men could hear the Dutchman's voice – Mark's father – on the other end of the line. It was the older man's tone, however, which really struck them all, and made them nervous.

"Go," Mark said.

"CAT-2 has reported that the number of captives is in the range of

30,000–"

"My God!" Aaron gasped.

"–and there's just no way we're going to get them all out."

"How many can we get?" Mark asked over the radio.

"Right now we've got as many as we can rushing to the underground platforms, to awaiting trains sent in from the other bases."

"Where does that leave us?"

The men of CAT-3 stared at their commander in awe, and especially the calm he was displaying under pressure.

"In a good position to get as far into that base as possible, do the most damage as possible, and in the least amount of time possible."

"And captives?"

"Save as many as you can – orders are to blow the base at the hour."

"We read you, sir," Mark said, then the father and son signed-off and the men were left standing on the circular vehicle ramp to Level 3, staring at one another and wondering what they'd do. Turn stepped forward.

"Sir," he said to Mark, "I can move the fastest, I can–"

Mark shook his head and put up his hand. "No, Turn – we need you with us, always." He looked to the others. "We all need to stay together, one false step or one side hallway and those Grays can have their way with you."

Turn nodded, for he fully understood what was at stake if the men were left alone – he'd seen it firsthand in Montana.

"This is what we'll do," Mark said as he started down the ramp again, his machine gun held out in case something should jump out at them, "Level 4 is coming up, and it's there that they do a lot of their experiments on humans…the ones they haven't changed physically yet. Our chances of making this mission mean something lie there."

"And Levels 5, 6 and 7?" Aaron asked.

Mark shook his head. "We'll never make it down to Level 7 where the train platforms are – we were never supposed to. Levels 5 and 6 are Nightmare Hall and the Hall of Horrors. If Walter and Charlie can make even the slightest of dents in those terrible operations then we've also got something to crow about."

"And if they don't?" Jerry asked.

Mark gave him a hard look. "Then the actions we take in the next few minutes will mean so much more." He looked down at his watch, frowned, then met their eyes again. "We've got twenty minutes, gentlemen – when that time is up this base is blown, whether we're topside or not."

37 – MATERIAL ACQUISITION TEAM

Dulce Entrance (Level 1)
Thursday, May 24, 1979

"Get down!"

The special forces soldier began to look up but then training took over and he pulled his head back instead. Some kind of laser bullet or blast struck the steel and cement wall and sent fragments of it flying about.

"Watch it!" Stu shouted back at him, though with this time a shake of the head.

Stu watched him turn his attention back to his covering fire, and however many Grays and Reptilians were still pouring forth. The few men of the Material Acquisition Team were fanned-out about the first level of the base, strategically placing explosives, anticipating the pull-out and ensuring they'd damn-well be ready for it…and damn sure they'd not have to come back again. Stu was one securing explosives, and that time he just got a little too carried away. Vowing to not place them so close to the active fire areas, he turned around to head back toward the port. Doing so, his eyes glanced down at the bits of wall that'd just been blown away. He cocked a brow and was about to turn away when something else caught his attention – a small panel set into the wall, something that looked like a compartment of some sort. Looking over to see Ronnie still firing away at some of the additional Reptilians that'd just arrived, Stu took the few steps to it and then bent down, prying his fingers around the edges. To his astonishment, the thing 'popped' right open, revealing that it was indeed a small compartment. And inside was–

"What's that?"

Stu turned about, his heart-skipping a beat.

"God – you scared me!" he said, seeing Stan standing there.

Stan scoffed, but ignored the words and instead pointed down at the now-open compartment and the small metallic object sitting there.

"What the hell is that thing?"

Stu frowned. "If it's what I think it is, then we'll want to get it back to the port area and secure it as fast as possible.

He put the device under his jacket and then hurried past Stan, back toward the port.

~~~

"What the hell is it?" Ronnie asked, looking down at the small device. It was small, round and metallic and looked like a landmine of some sort, although much shinier and expensive. The metal looked to be steel but had a blue sheen to it. On the very top, the highest point on the small dome-shaped device, was an electronic display of some sort, red letters just like the movies.

"Here's where it works," Stu said, turning it over. "Best I can tell it's a CED, kind of like a mini-nuke and a–"

"Whoa, doc…a nuke!"

"Take it easy, Ronnie," Stan said, putting his hand on the astronaut's shoulder, "let Stu here finish."

"A Cell-Electrostatic-Disruption, or CED device, is a weapon that can be set to disrupt the cells of a living creature at a subatomic level, thus killing everything living in an area without doing much harm to any structures or equipment. It's kind of like a mini-nuke and an electromagnetic pulse all rolled into one, though with a much, much lower area of impact, discharge, and area of effect," Stu continued, giving Ronnie a sharp look on that last bit.

"What the hell's all that mean in English, doc?" Ronnie said with a laugh.

"It'll destroy every living thing in this base all the way to the deepest levels, even the ones we don't know about," Stu replied evenly, his eyes staring straight ahead at nothing, or perhaps at what such a cataclysmic event would look like.

"That's what we need," Ronnie said with a nod. He started forward and reached down to take the device from Stu. "How do we start it and where does it need to go?"

Stu jerked his arms, recoiling from Ronnie's advancing hands. "*I'll* take care of it."

Ronnie gave him a hard look, but bit his lip and nodded, then looked back to the port.

"Saddle up," he said, "we're gonna be gettin' the hell out of here real soon I have a feeling."

38 – BREAKING RANKS

Dulce Tunnels (Level 2)
Thursday, May 24, 1979

The men moved forward, Mark and Turn in the lead. Ahead was a fork, a crossroads of sorts, where two of the tunnels branched-off.

"Hear that?" Turn said, glancing over at Mark.

"Faintly," Mark replied.

The men waited a moment and when the others caught up they noticed how they began to look about, as if they too were hearing something.

"Women," Turn said, "they've got them down…both of these tunnels, by the sound of it."

"You've got good legs *and* good ears?" Aaron asked with a laugh. Turn just smiled and nodded.

"We've got to split up then," Mark said.

"Whoa, but–"

"No buts," Mark said, giving Aaron a hard look. "We've no super soldiers so we're all in the same boat here. We can, however save as many as we're able." The men nodded, and Mark pressed on. "Here's how we'll do it – Jerry and Billy and I will head down this left tunnel and the rest of you will head down the other, Aaron in the lead."

Mark looked to Turn, Andy and Johnny and they nodded. Then he looked to Aaron, who nodded as well.

The men went their separate ways.

~~~

"Over here," Mark said, waving his free hand and holding up his .45 with the other. The men had just turned a corner, shortly after separating from the others. Jerry and Billy looked and nodded – ahead of them were rows and rows of tall medical cabinets, their design looking to be from the 1950s or so. Ahead was a fork in the path, where a scientist or alien or–

A Gray stepped out and Mark knew immediately that it'd tried a mental attack, and failed miserably. His .45 boomed out at the same time Billy's and Jerry's machine guns did the same.

The men held their eyes on the sights of their guns, ready for–

Two more Grays stepped out, and again the three guns fired to life, the sound echoing wildly in the large room, the old metal cabinets amplifying it ten-fold.

"Three," Billy said. "How many more you think they'll send?"

"I don't know," Mark said, and he got up the few feet needed to make it to the fork. It was clear, and he glanced back at the two. His eyes immediately went wide.

"Watch out!"

It was too late. Both Jerry and Billy turned around just in time to see the Reptilian swiping it's clawed hand forward. Jerry's glasses flew off and hit the floor, and a split second later were sprayed with their former owner's blood. Billy's eyes went wide and he pulled up his machine gun and began firing, the sight of Jerry's face ripped from his head nearly making him sick.

"Aaahhh!" he screamed firing continuously into the Reptilian's body. Mark fired at another coming up on them, and then rushed to Billy and grabbed him by the shoulder.

"Stop!" he shouted, and Billy did so, though he looked on the verge of tears. Both men looked down to see the clawed-hand of the Reptilian still embedded in the pulpy mass where Jerry's face had been. Billy bent over and started to retch and Mark frowned.

"C'mon," he said, getting one of Billy's arms around his shoulder, "let's get back to the port."

~~~

The four men rushed forth, Turn in the lead. They rounded a bend and Turn looked both ways. It was clear. They just had to get–

BOOM!

The blast left the men dazed, and Turn on the floor. There was a ringing in his ears and a strong sense of déjà vu. He just happened to be looking forward, toward the large bay doors that led out of the large open area of Level 4 and back onto the road that led further down into the base. And there was Andy, more than fifty yards away now, and nearly to the doors.

"No, Andy!" Turn shouted, but it was no use – Andy was crazy with hysteria, fear and panic. There was no talking sense into him, but there still was a chance to save him. Turn looked over at Aaron, who gave the slightest of nods. Turn was already two dozen yards away by the time his chin stopped moving.

"You can't…" Johnny said, still lying on the floor, dazed from the blast.

"We can't leave a man behind," Aaron said, then moved closer to his fallen comrade.

Ahead of them Turn's cybernetic legs were more than a match for Andy's human variety, and he caught up with him just as they crossed through the bay doors.

"Easy, Andy," Turn said, grasping him by the shoulders and turning him around. Andy's breathing was frantic and his eyes were wide – it was clear to Turn that he was in shock. "Listen, we've got to get–"

BOOM!

Turn didn't know what it was, but it felt like some kind of blast of air that'd knocked him down. All he knew was that he was on the floor, on his side, and staring across the long, open floor of Level 4, right back at Aaron, who was slowly pulling a bloody knife from Johnny's chest. Aaron looked up at just that moment and their eyes met, Turn's going wide.

He whipped his gaze away, to his right, and saw Andy lying there, his head a bloody mess from where it'd hit the wall or floor or…something. Turn scurried over to him and immediately saw he was dead. He glanced back at Aaron, who was now wiping the blood from his knife onto Johnny's clothing. Turn thought he'd be sick, like he would after someone had given him a swift kick in the gut. Instead he pushed himself to his feet and watched as Aaron put the large Bowie knife back in his leg-sheath and reached for the two 9mm handguns at his waist.

Turn gripped the stock of his AR-15, two choices before him. He took the second, he ran deeper into Dulce.

39 – OVERRUN

Dulce Tunnels (Level 6)
Thursday, May 24, 1979

"Aaahhh!" John yelled, his finger held down on the AR-15 machine gun's trigger until it went click. He looked down at it for a brief moment, grabbed a grenade from the front of his jacket, and hurled it at the now-regrouping Reptilians.

BOOM!

"Reptilian soup," Charlie said beside him, and John looked over from beneath his helmet just in time to see him cock an eyebrow. Resisting the urge to laugh at how absurd it all was, John let the machine gun fall to hang by its strap from his neck and grabbed the 9mm at his side.

Charlie saw none of that, for he'd turned his attention back to the hallway that led back to the tube train platform, the spot he hoped to hell Donlon and his CAT-4 team was still defending. The alternative was too grim to think on, especially when they were this close. After Walter had run on they'd fought their way back from the Hall of Horrors and that was no understatement. The Grays of the base, realizing they had a good chance of being overrun now that they'd been caught with their pants down, had largely disappeared. That didn't mean things were any easier, it just meant that now there seemed to be a dozen Reptilians for each and every Gray they'd seen before. And whereas the Grays were relatively easy to kill – slow reaction times, frail bodies, and little defensive capabilities when the super soldiers were present – the Reptilians were fighters through and through. *Thank God they can't do mind attacks*, he thought to himself for what seemed like the hundredth time as they turned another corner and he lit into another group of the things, his twin Colt .45s laying them down with holes through their skulls.

Beside him John wondered if the other teams were suffering as much as theirs had. They'd lost their two super soldiers, both in the same freak attack, and the pessimist in him told him that wasn't something confined to his team alone. It was almost as if they'd been set up, but even that was too far for his negative way of looking at things, for the moment at least.

"There!" Charlie said, drawing John's attention back just as he'd been snapping another ammo clip into his AR15. Sure enough, it was the entrance to the tube station platform…and…

"It's gunfire," Charlie said, as if reading his thoughts, "Donlon and his boys are still holding."

John nodded, hoping it was true, but knowing seeing was believing as well, plus–

"Back!" Charlie hissed, trying to keep as quiet as he could but startled by what he'd seen. Down the slight incline in the tunnel was a whole nest of aliens – a half-dozen Reptilians, two Grays, and one especially large Gray, the kind with long spindly arms and a height that caused it to hunch over lest it hit its massive head on the ceiling. He and John immediately jumped back and got around a corner in the tunnel-hallway.

"What the hell is that thing?" John asked.

Charlie bit his lip, but answered. "It's those taller Type-B Bellatrax Grays, the ones Stan was talking about in that boring-as-hell briefing."

"Well…can we kill it?"

"You bet – so long as they don't detect us."

John frowned. At least that last grenade of his had taken the Reptilians off their tail…for however long that would last. Now they had ten or so aliens ahead of them – three of them most likely mind attackers, as he thought of the Gray bastards as.

"What'll we do?" he asked finally.

Charlie smiled. "Come on in here and listen."

40 – ALL IS LOST

Dulce Platform (Level 7)
Thursday, May 24, 1979

Colonel Roger Donlon stood there taking it all in and shook his head before wiping the sweat from his brow. A thousand – he'd lost count at a thousand. That's how many women he'd seen coming running back from the tunnels CAT-1 and CAT-2 had headed down. Most were young, naked and scared out of their minds. Robbie, David and Fred had been more shocked by them than the initial Gray and Reptilian assault they'd had to deal with, and Donlon had felt about the same. They'd quickly come to and Robbie and Fred had begun corralling the women onto the one usable tube train they still had. That'd filled up in seconds it'd seemed, and then they'd jiggered the controls to send it shooting off toward New York, the one spot Donlon had been told would be secure.

The call from General Anderholt hadn't come through on the satellite radio until the train had nearly filled up...almost like he'd had a camera and was watching them. Donlon had shaken the thought off immediately, especially when the general had told him another train would be shooting off to Los Angeles, all the men had to do was fill the next in line, the ones the Grays had been riding in on to kill them from just a short time before. They'd filled it even faster than the first before sending it off, and then another one was filled and shot off to Las Vegas. And so the process had repeated itself, again and again, until they were on their last train, this one only half-full, the tide of women now finally finished. Donlon looked back to the tunnels where the other teams had gone, and which were now blocked by a small group of Reptilians and a few Grays. At least the trains bringing in alien reinforcements had slowed, slowed considerably. Donlon figured they'd gotten wise to what they were up against, namely David's and

138

Fred's M203 grenade launchers, which were blowing each train's occupants to smithereens as soon as the doors gave their jolly jingle and opened up. It was a slaughter, plain and simple…but now they were out of grenades.

"Getting low on the Ingrams," Robbie said from where the men were now bunched up near some crates they'd dragged together, near the last half-filled train of screaming women.

"And about out of machine gun rounds too," David said.

Donlon nodded and looked to Fred. "Get that train out of here – no more women are coming now."

Fred nodded and got to it, and less than a minute later he was back with them on the platform, the train steadily gaining speed as it headed off toward New York or California or wherever – the men had lost track. They were tired, but holding, and Donlon could only hope the other teams were doing as well as they, not a scratch on any of them, their super soldier thwarting whatever attacks the Grays were trying to hurl their way.

"Let's break the flashguns out on their asses!" Robbie shouted. "What the hell else we gonna do?"

Donlon frowned but didn't disagree. As Bobbie spit some tobacco on the floor and said, 'what the hell else were they gonna do?'

"Alright," he said, then reached down and grabbed the flashgun, which he'd taken from a dead Gray's hand during one of the brief respites they'd had since they'd been on the platform. It'd been the only one in sight, and he hoped it'd help them now. He tossed it up to Robbie.

"Here goes," Robbie said after a moment, then fired the first blast, using the top button, vaporize. The beam hit one of the Reptilians in the mouth of the tunnel and immediately the creature puffed out of existence, a split-second spark and cloud and then just the black falling ash, a perfect little mound of the stuff rising perhaps an inch off the tunnel floor.

The other beasts howled and hissed their displeasure, and some of them even started gnashing their teeth and biting at each other, as if they were communicating their discontent, and desire to get away. The loss of a single one of their number to the flashgun just slowed the things, however, and the assault they looked ready to launch seemed all the more imminent.

"Open up on 'em!" Roger yelled as he too reached down for his 9mm and the men began firing away with what they had while Robbie did so with his, puffs of smoke and mounds of ash soon appearing in the alien's midst.

"Sir," Robbie said to Donlon, drawing his attention. The commander looked to his super soldier and nodded, and Robbie pressed on. "Sir, don't you think that we should—"

THUNK!

It came out of nowhere, a flying piece of debris, a rectangular piece of wall paneling not much larger than a shoebox top or…something. And now there it was, sticking from Robbie's head from where it'd impaled itself inches deep. Robbie's eyes glazed over and he dropped forward, dead, the flashgun skittering across the floor.

"Fuck!" Fred shouted and at the same moment David shouted "down!"

The three men dove down, but it did little good. A moment later all three began to float upward, their arms and legs locked at their sides, their bodies at the whim of something else's mind. What's more, they could hear the sound of another train coming in…and just as they began to float toward the tracks. Fred made to scream, but even their voices were powerless to them.

~~~

"Now!" Charlie half-whispered, half-yelled, and he and John both threw their remaining four grenades at the same time and then dove backward for cover. At the mouth of the tunnel ahead of them, the portion that led right to the train platform, the large, Bellatrax Gray looked down and immediately lost all mental focus at what it saw.

BOOM!

~~~

Donlon, David and Fred all three dropped at the same moment, hitting the station platform hard. They just happened to land so they were facing the mouth of the tunnel, and they therefore had quite the view of the explosion that killed the nest of aliens there. First the half-dozen Reptilians were eviscerated, though a few arms and legs and in once case a head, still flew out. Next the two smaller Grays were smashed into the wall, their heads exploding from the force. Finally, the largest of the Grays, the one with long spindly arms and a hunched over frame, seemed to just blast apart, one limb going in each direction. The men saw it all and couldn't believe it, not until Charlie and John appeared through the smoke and carnage. When they saw the tube train slide to a stop beside them, the doors chiming open, they knew they had a chance still of making it out of there.

Then the five Bellatrax Grays stepped out.

41 – FIRING 'ER UP

Dulce Entrance (Level 1)
Thursday, May 24, 1979

"C'mon!" Mark shouted as he hoisted one of the women up and over his shoulder then pulled the other one forward, the one that could still walk. She staggered ahead and he wheeled about to face the Reptilians on his tail again, his machine gun up and spraying out a steady arc of bullets. Several of the creatures fell, but several more bounded over the corpses to take their place.

Nearby was Billy, firing as well, and towing two females to top it off. In fact, each of the five or six times Billy, Jerry, and he had come in and out since splitting up with the others had resulted in them towing at least two women captives, if not more. The thought nearly made Mark shake his head, especially when he thought back to Jerry carrying one on each shoulder earlier on one of their many incursions into and then out of the tunnels, getting as many of the fleeing women as they could. Mark chuckled inside when he thought back to the women on Jerry's shoulders, each with one of the men's spare 9mm's firing away. It worked for moving fast, but Mark was unsure how many of the creatures the women hit. But then what did it matter? The call to go would come anytime now...had already, *hadn't it?*

At the time they hadn't know where all the women had been coming from, just that they were coming and that they had to save them. It was only when Mark began to question them further that he learned they'd run up all the way from the lower levels. The reason, he'd pressed them, was that fighting had broken out there. What's more, several of the women had said the Grays were pulling back, or better yet, nowhere to be seen. Still, there were more than enough Reptilians to make up for it, though at least they didn't have the ability to lift you into the air and smash your head against the wall like the Grays did.

Mark fought on, moving and turning about to fire and then moving some more. He was taking up the rear and he was beginning to feel that this would be the last run in, the last any of the team members could chance going back for anymore of the captives. Already they'd gotten hundreds – *hell, maybe thousands*, he thought when he remembered the call that'd come from General Anderholt and how he'd mentioned they were pulling out women left and right on the tube trains down below. It'd been mentioned, but there was no real way to know for sure. And how many women the aliens had in the depths of Dulce, women that were perhaps on even deeper levels and who'd never be discovered? Mark didn't want to think about that terrible thought.

He wheeled around again and fired off another burst, then reached down and grabbed one of the grenades at his belt and threw it too. He was already a good ten feet closer to the port when the thing went off behind him, the screeching of the dying Reptilians echoing up to reach him.

"Captain!" someone shouted, and Mark looked over to his left to see Aaron coming up from the same tunnel the two teams had separated at before.

Mark narrowed his eyes. "Where are the others?"

Aaron shook his head. "Johnny's dead – Reptilian got him with its claws. Andy saw it and got spooked, ran off into the base. Turn ran after him, there was some explosion, and then…" Aaron shook his head, clearly in shock over what'd happened, "…and then…they're gone, sir – they're just gone."

Mark nodded. "Where, Major?"

Aaron shook his head again, but Mark was having none of that. "Take me to the spot," he said, "I'm not leaving any men behind."

Aaron grabbed him by the arm as he tried to pass, and gave him a hard look. "They're dead, and you will be too if we don't get out of here, we all will be – who the hell is gonna fly that thing."

He nodded toward the bruised and battered X-22 still sitting near the downed-UFO. Mark held his gaze his jaw firm and near-quivering from anger, then looked over at the craft. Aaron was right, and he knew it. He looked back at the Major and nodded.

"Alright," he said, "let's get the hell out of here."

~~~

BOOM!

"Yee-haw!" Eddie shouted, pulling up on the controls of the alien fighter craft at the same time. He easily sailed up into a steep arc, then flipped the craft over so he was upright again and shot back toward the open port doors and the safety of the desert. Below him and in his wake was a smoking crater, the burned and shredded remains of more than a dozen Reptilians laying haphazardly about.

~~~

Moses wiped the sweat from his brow and shook his head. *That was close,* he thought, watching the alien fighter craft that Eddie was piloting fly back out into the desert, hopefully for another pass into the port, he told himself. Beside him Stan was still in the midst of reloading one of his Colt .45s.

"We've got to make a break for it," he said.

Stan scoffed, but didn't look up, just kept his eyes on the bullets that went steadily, one after another, into his gun. "We ain't goin' nowhere until Captain Richards gets back and gets that X-22 airborne."

"You think that thing's flying again?"

Stan looked up at him this time. "I don't think – I know."

"Oh yeah, and how you figure that?"

Stan flicked his chin toward the open port floor. "Because here he comes now."

Moses' eyes narrowed and he chanced sticking his head out. Sure enough, there was Mark, a couple more women on his arms and Billy and Aaron on his heels. He was pointing at the X-22, and Moses knew he meant to take it.

"Well, what are we waiting for?" he asked. "Let's give 'em a hand!"

~~~

"There she is!" Mark shouted over the continual firing. Andy and Aaron looked, and sure enough, there was the X-22, bruised and battered and blackened, but upright and looking ready to fly still. Mark nodded at it, raised his gun, hefted the women further up on his shoulders, and started forward

~~~

"Go, damn it!" General Anderholt shouted at the pilot.

"I'm going!" the Dutchman shouted back, clutching the controls of the Puma helicopter tightly, trying to keep it level in the growing desert wind. A storm was coming, an early morning storm – the horizon said it all, for it'd be red and orange and death incarnate come morning.

"Go, go, go!" Anderholt shouted, slapping his hand down on his leg.

"This bird can't go much faster," Ellis said as he looked over at the

General, "and besides—"

"Holy shit!" Anderholt shouted, his eyes going wide and his finger going to toward the cockpit window. Ellis shot his own gaze back.

"Oh, shit!" he said. A debt had come due.

42 – FROM ABOVE

Dulce Port (Level 1)
Friday, May 25, 1979

In the cockpit of the X-22, Mark stared out and knew that this was it, he and his men and the few women they'd saved were all dead. Glancing down at his watch he saw that it was just past midnight, and now hundreds of Reptilians were rushing forth from the HUB doors, the beasts' teeth gnashing and eyes filled with bloodlust. It'd only be a minute and they'd have the X-22 overrun, the doors pried open with their razor-sharp claws. All Mark could do was stare out the window and watch it happen, maybe take a few with his 9mm before he was overpowered.

With covering fire from Moses and Stan near the Puma transport helicopter, Mark and the others had been able to get across the huge port floor, Reptilian bullets and flashguns flying, but thankfully missing. They'd made it to the command facility, reloaded and took off again. From there it was a short distance to the X-22, and there were fewer aliens to contend with, and no Grays to speak of, thank God.

The radar blipped, and Mark's eyes shot down to the X-22's controls. Something was coming in, something big.

"Captain," Billy said from behind him, looking worried and pointing up, "we've got company."

~~~

From overhead a Sirian came down, in perfect sight of the helicopter piloted by the Dutchman more than a dozen miles away. It descended slowly from the stormy clouds, lightning accompanying it, its prow turning all the while, the sharp triangle coming slowly forward to face the open Port doors.

No one inside that port could see inside the craft, but there were Sirians there, friends of the Richards' from their off-world excursions, things many of the highest-level members of the government knew nothing about…many, but not all.

The craft angled in, and the Reptilians rushing forth on the floor of the port saw it, knew it, and shrieked. Their teeth gnashed something fierce, they broke ranks, and ran.

The first shot from the immense craft fired at just that moment, tearing into their scattered line and throwing the beasts every which way. They howled, and another blast came, blue-lighting in a ball and devastating, turning whole beings into pieces with every hit.

The craft hovered outside the port doors of Dulce for a manner of moments, and then ascended into the clouds just as quickly as it'd come down. The storm that'd been descending upon that area of New Mexico going with it.

43 – OUTTA THERE

"Who was that?" Billy shouted from the back of the X-22, but Mark ignored him, although he couldn't help the slight smile that edged onto one corner of his mouth. *They remembered*, he thought, *they remembered!*

Mark steeled his resolved and started hitting the controls. A moment ago there'd been hundreds of Reptilians pouring forth at them from the HUB doors. Now there were just a few straggling to get back in those doors, the vast majority of their comrades lying in pieces on the floor around them. Most of the fighter craft at that end of the port were also destroyed and the security facility was charred and blackened.

"Can we make it, Captain?" Aaron asked, coming up behind his seat.

"We can now, now that we're not gonna be eaten alive."

Aaron gulped. He hadn't imagined it'd be that bad.

"We're going home, boys!" he shouted out, then hit the final control that started up the X-22. The engines fired to life and the men in back cheered, the women wailing and crying in joy.

It took just seconds and the X-22 was up and pointing back around at the ruined port doors. Mark fired the engines and sent her out, toward Moses and the chopper with the rest of the men and rescued captives.

"If you're gonna blow her, now's the time!" Mark shouted back, and in the back, Stu stood up. He'd been quiet so far, and was quiet still when he took out the control to the Cell-Electrostatic-Disruption, or CED device, and looked at the men. He looked ready to say something, then sighed and shrugged. What was there to say? He pushed the button and the men all got up to rush to the small windows near the door, affording them a view back at the base.

"Nothing happened," Billy said.

"Maybe it needs a minute," Stu said.

"Or it could just be that—"

FFF…FFF…ZZZZ – ZAP!

Billy's words were cut off by the sound, and what came next. It was like some force had descended upon them, one that had their fingers tingling and their hair standing on end. The closest any of them could compare it to was an electromagnetic pulse, and that's about what this looked like. There was a thrum of some sort, one that built from the bottom of the base and then shot outward, like a sonic boom that couldn't be heard or seen, only felt. It created a short, sharp light, blinding in intensity but just for a moment. Then there was nothing.

"I don't think—"

BOOM!

Like ten sonic booms, the force of the blast made everyone involuntarily put their hands to their ears, even Mark flying the X-22. Below, Dulce Base seemed to lift up off the ground for the briefest of moments, although every man there knew something like that just wasn't physically possible. But then there were a lot of things in Dulce that weren't supposed to be physically possible.

The base never moved but all life inside of it did, to wherever it is that life from other parts of the universe, life engineered in labs, and life from the darkest recesses of our minds is ever capable of going. In a split-second every particle of every living cell in Dulce was atomized, ripped apart, and decimated.

"Hot damn!" Billy shouted.

Ahead in the cockpit, Mark smiled. Dulce was no more, and he was just meeting up with another helicopter, one flown by his father. The terror was over.

EPILOGUE – TURNING BACK

Dulce Tunnels (Level 5)
Thursday, May 24, 1979

Turn ran, his breathing frantic not because of his pace – he could run on his cybernetic legs for hours and not get tired like that – but because of that look on Aaron's face. He'd known what he'd done, he'd known and he'd been planning it. *What is going* on? Turn kept thinking as he ran further into the base. *What mission within a mission have I run into?*

He finally slowed, he didn't know where, somewhere on the edge of Level 5. It dawned on him that he hadn't seen a single Gray, nor a single Reptilian. There wasn't a single captive about either. It was quiet, too–

"Psst!"

Turn spun around and saw a wild-eyed man, his red, curly hair a stark contrast to those shining white teeth staring back at him. He was still several yards away, and hesitant, as if he'd just startled a wild animal and wasn't sure if he should try to be nice or try to run.

"Who the hell are you!" Turn nearly shouted, spooked more than he cared to let on.

"My name's Paul Benowitz, Turn, and you need to come with me – you need to come with me now, if you want to live."

Turn looked, narrowed his eyes.

"Man, I don't know who the hell you are! Why would you think I'd come with you?"

"Because you don't have much choice," a familiar voice came from behind, and Turn wheeled around to see Walter coming up.

"In about five minutes Stu's gonna trigger his device, blowing this base right to hell…or at least any life in it." Walter's eyes were locked right on Turn as he said the words, and he walked steadily forward. Not once did he

149

even glance at this new man...Benowitz."

"Aaron," Turn said, "Aaron—"

"Betrayed you, I know."

Turn's eyes narrowed again. "You know, how could you—"

"Turn – we don't have time!" Walter said, grabbing him forcefully by the arm as he started to walk forward, Benowitz doing the same.

"I'm not going!" Turn shouted, and easily slipped out of the grip.

"Fine," Walter said, and turned around to walk back into the tunnel from which he'd came, Benowitz right at his side.

Turn watched them go and it suddenly hit him, the truth, and so hard that his eyes began to water. Ahead Benowitz seemed to sense this – there was no way he could see from that far away...*was there?* – and he raised his arm up and gave a flicking motion with his hand, one that said 'c'mon!'

Turn turned back and looked in the direction where he'd last seen Mark and the rest of the men of CAT-3...and Aaron, and Johnny...he looked back where they had gone, then back at Benowitz, standing there and waving him on, a smile on his face, and Walter still walking on, though glancing back over his shoulder now. The bastards knew something, knew some secret that no one else did, or if they did, were too afraid to admit, even to themselves. *What was it?* Turn wondered, *and what...*

"Turn...Turn – c'mon!" a shout came from further up ahead, through the tunnel and where his companions had gone. It was Aaron, Turn could tell.

Turn looked back, gritted his teeth, then dashed forward. He ran toward...Paul Benowitz, and the deepest recesses of Dulce, its darkest secrets yet...and maybe, just maybe, a little of whatever truth the secret underground alien base still held.

To Be Continued...

ABOUT THE AUTHOR

Greg Strandberg was born and raised in Helena, Montana, and graduated from the University of Montana in 2008 with a BA in History. He lived and worked in China following the collapse of the American economy. After five years he moved back to Montana where he now lives with his wife and young son. He's written more than 50 books.

26315526R00091

Made in the USA
San Bernardino, CA
24 November 2015